Lost Hound

Robert L. Ashcom, MFH

LOST HOUND

AND OTHER HUNTING STORIES AND POEMS

BY
ROBERT L. ASHCOM

Illustrations by Jane Gaston
Frontispiece by Sandra Massie Forbush
Foreword by James L. Young, MFH

THE DERRYDALE PRESS

MILLWOOD HOUSE

1999

THE DERRYDALE PRESS

Published in the United States of America
by The Derrydale Press and Millwood House, Ltd.
4720 Boston Way, Lanham, Maryland 20706

Distributed by NATIONAL BOOK NETWORK, INC.

Copyright © 1999 by Robert L. Ashcom (text)
Jane Gaston (chapter illustration)
Sandra Massie Forbush (frontispiece illustration)
First cloth printing 1999

All rights reserved. No part of this publication may be reproduced, stored in a retrieval system, or transmitted in any form or by any means, electronic, mechanical, photocopying, recording, or otherwise, without the prior permission of the publisher.

British Library Cataloguing in Publication Information Available

Library of Congress Cataloging-in-Publication Data

Ashcom, Robert L.,
    Lost Hound : and other hunting stories and poems / by Robert L. Ashcom ; illustrations by Jane Gaston ; frontispiece by Sandra Massie Forbush ; foreword by James L. Young.
        p. cm.
   ISBN 1-56416-173-0 (alk. paper)
   ISBN 1-56416-176-5 (leatherbound)
   1. Fox hunting—Virginia—Literary collections. 2. Fox hunting—Virginia—History. I. Title
   PS3551.S366 L67 1999
   811'.54—dc21   99-046004
                                               CIP

♾™ The paper used in this publication meets the minimum requirements of American National Standard for Information Sciences—Permanence of Paper for Printed Library Materials, ANSI/NISO Z39.48-1992.
Manufactured in the United States of America.

This book
is for Susie

who has been with me
on night searches
for more than just hounds

with all my love

Acknowledgements

As is customary in such documents, I must begin by saying that it is impossible to name all the people who, over the years, have helped me in the journey I have taken through the world of hunting into the larger world of the life of the countryside. But certain names stand out: the names of the huntsmen behind whom I have ridden; and who, in many cases, have answered my questions in long conversations over the telephone.

I begin with A.C. "Curt" Dutton, longtime huntsman to the Mission Valley. Even over the span of the years I remember Curt as a patient soul who put up with my impatience and who, on many occasions, said to me (when I was not supposed to be whipping-in), "Ride on out there and see what happens, but don't let anybody see you." In that way I learned my first lessons in hunting, by being in front of everything and being careful not to let anybody see me. It was there that Susie and I began our lives with Fluter. And the part of his story with the coyote took place at Mission Valley. Curt had a curious gurgling sound he used when the hounds were drawing. I took it up, and so remembered Curt each time I began to draw with a pack.

After various intervening adventures, we arrived back at home in Charlottesville, Virginia, and for three seasons I was field master behind

Jack Eicher at Farmington. Being field master when you aren't the MFH (and, hence, have no ultimate responsibilities) is, in many ways, the most enjoyable job on a hunt staff. It leaves plenty of time for watching what the huntsman is doing. It is a classroom with an unobstructed view of the teacher. In the field, I learned from Jack attention to detail—every detail, and learned that every crow call and every running rabbit and all the tracks on the paths had their tales to tell, and in that tough country, you'd better understand them.

Next is Buster Chadwell. I only spent one day with Buster at the Essex, but it was the best hunting day of my life. The hunt lasted virtually all day. Trying and hunting and running, on and on. I had Fluter, and—as I am fond of saying—time really did stop. Buster was kind to me when there wasn't much reason to be. And when we went to western North Carolina, he spent an inordinate amount of time explaining the Essex breeding which had preceded me there. He was the gentlest huntsman I ever saw. And maybe the gentlest man I ever saw. I revere his memory.

Behind all of this and still feeling like a friendly ghost over my writing table is Albert Poe. Once, when a number of us were at dinner at the Virginia Hound Show, someone asked the group at large how on earth a person could learn to be a huntsman in this day and age. Albert, without hesitation, said, "I taught Bobby Ashcom how to do it over the phone." There was laughter. But there was also more than a grain of truth in it. My first hounds came from Albert when he was at Piedmont, and the last hounds I hunted were largely the same breeding. The names Render, Charter, Workman, Rustic, Ruby, Essex Fireman, Green Spring Valley Poacher, and on and on, are the names etched on my hunting memory. They are a part of every hound I ever bred—beginning in 1968 and arcing across all the intervening years. That the American hound seems to be in a difficult corner these days is not to minimize the talents and dedication of many current huntsmen and masters, myself included. Rather, it is to say that there has not recently been a hound breeder with the resources and country upon which to practice an utterly superior understanding of the

Acknowledgements

nature of the foxhound—like Albert Poe. The Piedmont packs of the early seventies and late sixties were by all accounts among the most impressive of the second half of the twentieth century. Let one example suffice. A hunt was described to me in which the pack came over the crest of a hill tightly bunched up—as if they were a single organism. About 40 hounds. The fox a quarter of a mile ahead. There was a page wire fence halfway down the hill. There was a strand of barbed wire over the page wire. The bottom was tight to the ground. Room for the fox. None for the hounds. They flowed over the top of that fence like molten lava. And you could hear the staples zinging as the wire came loose from the posts because of the weight of the pack. Throwing their tongues all the while.

And so, dear reader, as you read these stories and poems, there will be a shadowy voice behind mine. The voice coaches me along as I try to unravel some of the mystery and humor and joy of our fast departing rural countryside, with all the traditions which have meant so much to so many of us. And when, for example, you read the part in "Turtle Hound" where my Ready (Albert had one, too) raises his head and calls, hear also the voice of Piedmont Charter as he raised his head so many times in the Piedmont country and called, and know that behind both voices is the patient, insistent voice of Albert Poe telling me the way the life of the countryside should be. And that I should believe him because he has seen it, with his own eyes.

Foreword

This collection of reminiscences, essays and poems by life-long foxhunter Robert Ashcom will entice, delight and intrigue the community of fox-chasers it targets. An eclectic melange of subjects, *Lost Hound* contains a quiet trove of serendipity to be savored in front of a fire with a retired foxhound or provided as bedside reading for foxhunting guests.

Bobby Ashcom grew up in Charlottesville, Virginia amongst ponies and fauna of similar ilk which obviously nurtured in him a sensitivity for animals and their homes. That acuteness has now evolved into this adroit inspection and introspection of his avocation. During the course of his varied career he has whipped-in at Mission Valley Hunt in Kansas; started his own pack, the Bradbury Foxhounds, in Massachusetts; served as Field Master at Farmington Hunt in Virginia; and completed his hunting career as huntsman and MFH at Tryon Hunt in North Carolina. He and his wife, Susan, now reside in Virginia where they both hunt with the Warrenton Hunt, and Bobby teaches at Fairfax Community College. Susie whips in to the Warrenton pack.

The apparent effect of all those positions is his sharpened focus on all of the subtleties of venatic interplay. *Lost Hound* reflects this sensitivity to the intricate fabric of venery.

Lost Hound

A significant supplement to Ashcom's hunting acumen is his literary experience—as both a published writer and a teacher of writing. His word-play reflects the hum of hunting and nature's feral heartbeat. Moreover, his meter and rhyme (Oh, that would-be Ovids would eschew "free verse.") sing praises to the disciplined, euphonic poesy of rigorous rhyme and syncopated reason!

> At dawn, at hillside's edge, the hounds and I,
> Beneath the faded morning moon, paused
> To hear the hunting wood-hawk's whistled cry
> And watch the silent, massive cornfield seem
> To leap from night to misty day and cause
> A sudden click, like waking from a dream.
>
> *The Gleaner*

Iambic pentameter—the stuff of Shakespeare! But also a rhyming scheme (abacbc)! Assonance! Imagery! His exacting creativity serves up a richness to the experience which we all can recognize.

There is an immediacy and intimacy to the vignettes and visions Ashcom offers up. New situations and settings, yes, yet they are familiar and nostalgic. His lines,

> Drawn taught in hunger's pull, circling down
> The wind to prove the ear's uneasy truce with fear

strike a resonant chord with any huntsman calling for a young hound left out after hunting. The crucible is when both hunters connect with relief.

> And in that moment's hush his eyes came clear,
> As if to make a mirror of my face.
>
> *Lost Hound*

Bobby Ashcom retains a certain wonder in his writings, enhanced by a very quiet humor and a Hemingway-esque sparseness to his prose.

Foreword

It was a shame to call such a horse Mule, but there you are.

Mule

The characters that emerge from the tapestry of his life with horse and hound are real and mystical, flawed and heroic, genuinely genuine.

Artist Jane Gaston, a native Virginian and accomplished equestrienne in several disciplines in her own right, illustrates with scenes and vignettes both evocative and poignant. Her work alone elevates *Lost Hound*, yet can stand apart as pure hunting art. She is a sensitive and spectacular artist with a broad spectrum of subjects, and her contributions to this volume only enrich it.

This little gem of a book is aimed at foxhunters, but it will touch a larger audience: any equine, sylvan or canine afficionado. It is broader and deeper than a treatise on hunting; rather, it is a touchstone for one's sporting sensibilities and a wellspring for the rural condition.

Indeed, the rural condition is imperiled by rampant development, and the fragile future of open space for pastoral sustenance is threatened. Bobby Ashcom awakens our awareness of the spiritual nourishment provided by the countryside where man's physical needs are tended by nature's guileless grandeur.

His thoughts might stir our soul; hopefully, they might also tweak our conscience.

> James L. Young, MFH
> Old Denton
> The Plains, Virginia
> June, 1999

Publisher's Foreword

Enthusiastic as I am about publishing this book, I am equally excited about what its publication represents: good times. The last decade of this century has been a good time for foxhunting literature. In 1994 the Masters of Foxhounds Association introduced their quarterly newsletter-magazine, *Covertside*. Its distribution grew quickly to almost 15,000 foxhunting enthusiasts. In 1990, Virginia retailer Marion Maggiolo began publication of *In & Around Horse Country*, a newspaper with an emphasis on foxhunting and steeplechase racing. These two publications have, over the past few years, provided vehicles through which a new generation of sporting writers have been able to reach a national audience—James L. Young, Henry Hooker, Tommy Lee Jones, Barclay Rives and, of course, the author of this collection, Robert Ashcom.

It hasn't always been this way. Foxhunting literature has thrived at best only in fits and starts over the last couple of centuries. From the time William Somervile wrote his epic poem, "The Chace" (1735), almost fifty years elapsed before Peter Beckford set down his *Thoughts on Foxhunting* (1781). Another fifty and more years passed before a handful of British sporting journalists and writers—Surtees, Nimrod, Scrutator, Wanderer—further developed the genre by producing their brilliant body of work.

Lost Hound

Although the sport of British-inspired foxhunting was practiced in the southern states of this country as early as the eighteenth century, American sporting literature didn't appear until the nineteenth century. Even then, most educated Americans in the northern states were engaged not in sport but in commerce or industry. Nineteenth century American writers, like soul mates Alcott, Emerson, Thoreau and Hawthorne, explored American social, philosophical and political themes. In the rural south of the nineteenth century, the small appetite for foxhunting literature was satisfied by periodicals such as the *American Turf Register and Sporting Magazine*; *Turf, Field and Farm*; *American Field* and *Scribner's*, which published articles by Joel Chandler Harris (later renowned as the author of the "Uncle Remus" stories), George L.F. Birdsong (breeder of the foxhound strain carrying his name), Col. Frederic Gustavus Skinner and others.

It wasn't until the first half of the twentieth century that American sporting literature achieved its first "golden age." A new generation of wealthy Americans emerged—many, the sons of the previous century's industrialists—with the financial means and the leisure time for recreation and sport. During this period, a few major publishers such as Alfred A. Knopf, Macmillan, Garden City, Scribner's and Doubleday published books by contemporary American sporting authors, and republished classic books by English authors, to satisfy a growing American interest in foxhunting. (Today, in our mass-market economy, no major publishing house can even consider publishing books for such a limited audience.) Small publishing houses were formed, dedicated specifically to a narrowly-defined sporting market. The Derrydale Press, founded in New York by Eugene V. Connett in 1927, began publishing high quality sporting books, poetry and art. Stacy Lloyd's Blue Ridge Press in Berryville, Virginia was another niche publisher of important sporting authors. Through these few mainstream general trade publishers and the small special-market publishers of that period, authors Joseph B. Thomas, David Gray, Gordon Grand, Mason Houghland, M. O'Malley Knott, J. Blan van Urk and A. Henry Higginson contributed to a new American body of foxhunting literature.

Publisher's Foreword

Shortages of high quality materials during World War II stifled Derrydale's endeavors, and the application of the nation's post-war energies to rebuilding the peace-time economy postponed the further development of American sporting literature. Fortunately, at about this time, a gifted individual, who could have succeeded at any career of his choice, succumbed totally to the seduction of the field and devoted his working life as well as his leisure time to equine sports and foxhunting. Alexander Mackay-Smith wrote, collected and produced a body of foxhunting literature practically single-handedly through much of the last half of the twentieth century. As editor of *The Chronicle of the Horse* for twenty-five years, and through his own books, Mackay-Smith provided foxhunting enthusiasts with sporting news, information, articles, scholarship, music, art and literature.

Peter Winants, then John Strassburger, followed Mackay-Smith as editors of the *Chronicle*, making their own substantial contributions, but the *Chronicle*'s mission during their tenures was broadening to provide coverage of new and expanding equine activities. Foxhunting as a subject, once the backbone of *Chronicle* content, fell to an ever diminishing portion of the magazine's coverage.

I like to think that, in this last decade of the twentieth century, *Covertside* and *In & Around Horse Country* have responded to fill a need for foxhunters, and are contributing to a resurgence in American foxhunting literature in two ways. First, by providing space in their pages for contemporary writers, they are enabling a new generation to be read. Second, by serving a narrowly-focused readership, they are providing a cost-efficient advertising medium for small specialty publishers like *Millwood House* and self-publishers like Nancy Hannum and Benjamin Hardaway to reach their potential readers.

Now in this final year of the twentieth century, the aforementioned Derrydale Press, the premier sporting publisher of the early twentieth century, has been resurrected by publisher and foxhunter Jed Lyons. In co-publishing this volume with Millwood House, the Derrydale Press embarks upon an ambitious plan to once again offer fine sporting literature, printed and bound in the best materials, the new as well as reprints of the classics, to the sportsmen and women of today and into the twenty-first century. Good times for the literate sportsman!

> Norman M. Fine
> The Clearing
> Millwood, Virginia
> August, 1999

Author's Note

ᚨ

This symbol, which appears at the end of each story, is the rune, "aesc," or ash (the tree), the ancient symbol for the first part of my name. It is from the alphabet used by the Norse peoples before the advent of the Romans. The runes are phonetic and have names, thus the "ash." They were thought to be magic in the right hands and as carved figures were "cast" to tell the future. The strokes of the runic letters are straight lines, suitable for cutting inscriptions into stone. As the Norsemen (the Vikings) passed through new territory (from New Brunswick to Constantinople), they "cut runes" into standing stones to memorialize their passing. In a way, in this book, I am also cutting runes. Finally, together with the old form "coombe," now spelled "com," my name means "ash valley."

Contents

Dedication v
Acknowledgments vii
Foreword by James L. Young, MFH xi
Publisher's Foreword xv
Author's Note xix

The Gleaner 1
The Chicken 5
The Well 13
Lost Hound 21
Dixie 25
How Wild Are Your Foxes? 33
The Old Hen in Fall 41
Why Hounds Hunt 45
Fluter 51
The Land 61
Old Ronda 71
Young Ronda 79
Turtle Hound 87
Foxhounds Asleep 95
Mule 99
Cows 107
Backfire 119
The Cat and the Swimming Pool 127
Cain's Song 135
Winter Run 147
The Blessing of the Hounds 159

The Gleaner

The Gleaner

At dawn, at hillside's edge, the hounds and I,
Beneath the faded morning moon, paused
To hear the hunting wood-hawk's whistled cry
And watch the silent, massive cornfield seem
To leap from night to misty day and cause
A sudden click, like waking from a dream.

Here at summer's final surge, the young
Fox finds on moisture-laden, glowing ground
The rabbit's track, and runs the line among
The towering stalks until the tale's end;
Then hides his catch and harkens to the sound
Of mice beneath a corn root's shallow bend.

And thus he hunts the cornfield's world until
He hears the old hounds strike, in dew-drenched grass,
His fading track at field's edge and spill
Like smoke into its hold, where the young
Ones catch the scent and drive ahead to pass
The wiser hounds and cry the track alone.

A puddle like a little lake lies deep
Within that field; and the knowing fox will chill
The puppies' joyous plunge—and leap
Into that barren pool—across and gone,
To hear, at hillside's edge, the hunt go still
And scratch a flea and cock his head and yawn.

Lost Hound

I knew that puddle, too, and puppies' pride
As well, so gave my horse to the Whip to hold
And thrashed into the cornfield's depth to chide
The young ones for their youth and set them straight
Across, so when the old hounds caught the cold
And sinking track, they'd hark to them without a check.

And in that breathless pause before the strike,
With the cornfield hushed to hear the ancient song,
We heard the Diesel's roar and smelled its smoke
And fled; for we did not own that field, and Time
Is Cash and the Gleaner's twelve foot swath along
The field's edge cuts clean our autumn hymn.

ᚠ

The Chicken

At many hunting establishments chickens are put out in certain places in the countryside for the foxes to eat. In a way I was doing the hens a favor. To end their lives in nature, away from the huge, mechanical laying houses and not in a pot pie or voodoo rite in the Caribbean (which one of my suppliers swore was always a real possibility) seemed fitting somehow. It was as if I were making some amend for the way the hens had spent their lives.

Usually these hens' flying feathers were non-existent. However, a flyer was not unknown, and for almost two years we had one loose around the kennel. When it became apparent that, in spite of the predators, this hen was going to survive, she began to acquire names—usually heroic ones. In the end, however, she became known to her fans as "Chicken" or, on more formal occasions, "The Chicken."

Angela, my kennel girl—who was in real life a writer of children's stories and "romances"—had a habit of leaving me detailed notes about the status of the hounds whenever I was away. She became quite partial to Chicken and would leave me notes about her also. Probably the most notable one was left after Chicken had apparently been mauled by a fox and was not feeling up to snuff. On this occasion the note, written in her precise hand, read, "'The Chicken' is not feeling well; please give her a shot." Surely a comment on our society.

Chicken survived because she learned to come in the main kennel door at night and hide behind the water tank. The outside predators would not come into the kennel; and she very quickly learned that the inside predators were behind bars, as it were; and that the two-legged variety found her rather fetching. She lived on dog food. Once we got to know this, she was given a little pile of food each morning. She molted and grew an impressive set of feathers, including flying feathers. This gave her more confidence, as she could now fly—at least to a certain extent.

Her relations with the hounds were amusing. When she figured out that they couldn't get her, she began to parade up and down the main aisle talking her growlly talk. At first the hounds were furious. But as time went on, they became philosophical, except for the youngest ones who thought they hated her bitterly. To make the situation even more stressful for the youngsters, she soon began to parade right next to the chain-link gates. As young noses—and old ones, too, in the beginning—were thrust through the wire, she would peck them, arousing a hopeless fury in the "peckee."

By the end of her first summer, Chicken was settled in. During this time there had been speculation as to what would happen if Chicken should happen to get into a pen with the hounds, and visiting ladies had been teased with the scenario of Chicken being torn to pieces by the vengeful hounds.

Because of our kennel routine, the possibility existed. The hounds were let out each day into the drawing yard while their runs and the sleeping rooms were hosed down. These rooms opened onto the main aisle, and Chicken liked to wander into them and pick around in the shavings on the benches, and generally supervise the routine. Angela was always careful to get her out of the runs before she let the hounds back in. Being an aware person, she had no problem with this responsibility.

On my day to do the kennel, however, I liked to do a lot of heavy duty thinking (some would say daydreaming) while I hosed the runs; and at the end of these sessions, I had to remind myself sharply not to forget Chicken. Of course the day came when, having finished filling the water tubs and shutting the inside gates, I opened the gate to the drawing yard and let the hounds in, not thinking a thing of it.

During the ensuing scene, there was no sound. It was as if the kennel run had become a bathtub with the hounds as the water, whirling around in a circle, getting ever closer to the center. As the swirl neared the vortex, it suddenly dawned on me what was happening. My first thoughts were not of the chicken but of what would happen to me if she got eaten. So I plunged into the fray and came up with a hen nearly drowned in hound slobber but without another mark on her. During her time with us, she had become a very confident bird, and as soon as I got her into the air, she began looking around in a hostile sort of way, making her "bwaak, bwaak," sound which meant she was secure and in control of the situation. The hounds thought she was wonderful.

The second time it happened, I was not so rattled and could pay attention to what was going on. It didn't seem to me that the hounds were really trying to kill her. It was more as if they wanted to sniff her and see what she was. However, I was never tempted to put her in with the hounds on purpose to see what would happen.

One evening that fall, I had to stay at the kennel to wait for a load of hay. I pulled my truck up next to the barn and settled back for the wait. Just in front of me, Chicken was pecking at insects in a bit of grass next to the heat pen house. Sassoon and another bitch were lying sprawled out on the concrete. The three of us were bemused by the hen as she pecked away, informing us by her clucking that everything was just fine, at least in her world. It was one of those scenes which you remember as a still life: the two bitches, me, the soft but quickened air of fall, and the hen, all caught up in a tableau.

The bitches and I were jerked from our reverie by a change in the hedge at the edge of the little lawn. There was a sudden darkening of a patch of honeysuckle, and a red fox's head emerged from the green leaves. The three of us saw him at once and went rigid—the bitches lying on their sides with raised heads, while I gripped the steering wheel with white knuckles. The hen, facing me, did not see the fox as he crept across the 20 feet separating them. I couldn't move, and the bitches didn't. Later, when I told the story to listeners, irate because I didn't intervene immediately, I made up the excuse that I was going to jump into it before the fox could kill her. But that's what it was—just an excuse. The two bitches and I might as well have been made of stone.

When the fox was 10 feet away from Chicken, he shot forward, about a foot off the ground, to catch the hen as she tried to fly. The bitches leapt up with a roar of fury and frustration, and I came to life, although I still didn't move. Chicken had her back to the fox. When she did see him, she instantly levitated herself 10 feet off the ground. She flew right towards the truck and then veered off, heading for the kennel and the water tank at high speed, producing sounds of fear and outrage.

Meanwhile, the fox became aware of the two hounds behind the chain-link fence. He immediately lost interest in the hen, stopped himself almost in mid-air, and whirled around to look at his would-be assailants. The bitches then went totally berserk and began to throw themselves against the fence in a manner that could only be judged insane. Back on the ground, the fox trotted towards them, his brush straight out behind him. Two feet from the wire, he turned and sat down, looking them right in the eye. Then, cutting through the sounds of hysteria, came the barking cough typical of two dog foxes in breeding season. In this case, however, there could be little doubt that the strange bark was one of sheer triumph.

The scene must have been short, because the fox could not afford to let down his guard to indulge in a cheap thrill for very long. Abruptly, he stopped barking and turned toward the truck, and saw me. It was as if, as the situation cooled, he began to tune in to his surroundings again. Without another glance, he turned and trotted across the grass and disappeared into the honeysuckle.

It was one of those experiences when you are left out of breath even though you haven't done anything. In a minute I opened the truck door and spoke to the bitches, who were out of breath for real.

The Chicken

The Chicken, when I walked into the kennel, had recovered completely and was striding up and down next to the gates in case some dumb hound should put out a nose to be pecked.

She died what in human terms would be called a good death. After she had been with us nearly two years, which would have made her about four, she began to lose her verve. There was not the same swagger to her gait as she patrolled the kennel aisle. And her appetite, which had always been voracious, began to leave her. Her whole system began to slow down. She spent more and more time sunning herself in a little patch of dust next to the heat-pen house. She had a characteristic pose which she struck when she was sunning. She would lie completely on her side with both legs stuck straight out, off the ground, and from this awkward position would bob and jerk her head and give a running commentary on what was going on around her. Toward the end, however, she stopped vocalizing while she was sunning. She would just lie there, without moving her head or saying anything.

Her slowing down caused much discussion among the staff and people who visited the kennel regularly. There were two schools of thought on what to do. The interventionists wanted to take her to the vet, put her on vitamins, administer vast amounts of antibiotics; in short, do something. The "let her be" school advocated doing nothing. The latter won out, and we determined to let nature take its course. She took to putting her head under her wing while sunning, and sometimes she didn't come inside in the afternoon.

One day, when I came back to the kennel at dusk, I noticed that she was still outside and went over to her; she was dead, and when I picked her up, I remarked to myself on how light she had become.

I took her to a place behind the kennel grounds, at the foot of Little Mountain, where two game trails cross, and left her. The next morning she was gone.

ᚠ

The Well

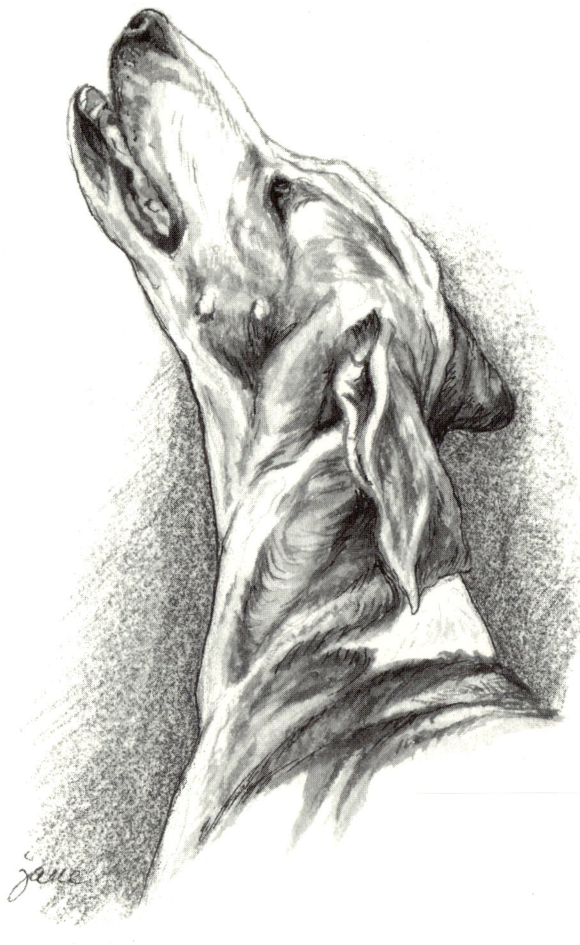

Some days you just feel centered—like the day is guaranteed. There is usually a sign: the coffee is really good; the traffic isn't awful; your secretary is smiling when you get to the office. During the winter, the sign for me was the smoke coming from the chimney of a certain house on the way to the kennel. On hunting mornings I was always glad to see it, because it seemed to hold some clue as to how the day would go. If the smoke was rising quickly and straight up, the day might be difficult. If it seemed to be actually falling, the same held true: for some reason the scenting would be bad. On the other hand, if the smoke was slowly but steadily rising from the chimney, often scenting would be good. Notice how I qualify my statements about scent. I'm not sure I know a lot more about it than I did 30 years ago. But one does pick up benchmarkers for the everyday questions of scent. But the whole picture? The constellation of factors governing scent seems to me to be so huge as to defy rational understanding. It ends up being a kind of mystery. Maybe that is one of the definitions of mystery. I have always liked mysteries.

So the smoke was good enough for me; and on the morning in question, it was just right. Almost no wind. Mid-thirties. Overcast. Moon the night before. Perfect hunting conditions for the creatures, including the fox. On

Lost Hound

I drove to the kennel. Loaded up fifteen couple in the trailer and went to the place of meeting, at the edge of a farm recently created from a very large tract. The new owners were planning to build a big house and a stable, but at this point it was just one 75 acre field sloping down toward a strong creek. With the field of riders close behind, I drew east, into a little breeze, through 20 acres of woods, toward a large tract of cut-over timber with the laps still down, but plenty of trails to get through on.

Immediately into the woods Spirit spoke. His most tentative calling note. The rest kept drawing, and I managed to keep my mouth shut. Then he spoke again and one of the old bitches went to him, and she spoke. I hurried down the trail to see if I could watch them: Okie was tracking along a log, and at the end she jumped off and both of them spoke. At which point I hollered and the rest came to see what it was all about. Across a broken-down wall and then alongside the wall they went, then off to the right toward the creek, feathering—no, the whole back end of each hound positively wiggling. And then they all opened. The people had caught up and were watching the drama. Whenever it happened, I felt like a party to a miracle. Also, for a second—at *least* for a second—I always thought that this would be the run of the century.

But reality set in. And the hounds threw up their heads just as they came to a gall spot at the beginning of the cow pasture—but cast themselves forward and hit it off again. Not hard, but going forward. It was like that for 15 minutes. Hounds patiently tracking up to the fox, with all of us behind full of anticipation. It was that kind of country. There wasn't a fox in every covert (sometimes not in every five coverts). So you had to hunt. You had to love to hunt. And if and when you finally struck it off, everyone—horses, people, hounds…everyone—was ready to go. That morning they struck well and hard, turned left-handed up a draw alongside a lake, heading for the cut-over, where they bobbled for a minute, and then went on toward State Line Church with a roar.

It was a good run. They went past the church to the swamp, made a full circuit, and lost the fox back at the church. It always surprised me that the hounds could run at all in that place. I once spent a couple of hours trying

The Well

to cross it on foot. The only way a fox could run in there would be to jump from hummock to hummock until the hounds were worn out from floundering after him. I drew on down through the woods to the bottoms. But we had had our run for the day, and were thankful, and ready to pick up the pack and head back to the meet. We went to Smothers's field to collect the hounds which weren't right with us. I blew and the whips counted. The wind had started to blow from the direction of the swamp, but we had almost all of them....

Missing two. Orvis came. Who was left? Look at the list. Roxanne? Totally unlike her! She was a little soldier, always there, no trouble. Did the whips miss her in counting? No. She wasn't here. Period. She might be back in the swamp, unable to hear me for the wind. Blow!

Send someone back to holler upwind. Twenty minutes went by. I was totally baffled—and worried. The whips all thought I was being my melodramatic self. A little switch had gone off in my head. Like the twitch you get when you are about to have a headache. I knew I had lost her. And I didn't know where!

But I did know that she hadn't just wandered off. Or split off on trash. Or done any of the many things which will cause a hound to get left out. Somehow I knew that.

I took the hounds to the kennel, fed, and went to lunch. Maybe I was overreacting. After all she was just a dog. We called her a hound, and she had a pedigree as long as your left leg, but so what? She was still just a dog. She would find her way home. That attitude didn't help. She was gone. I sat alone at lunch as was my habit. I slowly started to run the day past my mind's eye like a video tape. Maybe there was a clue there.

As I replayed the day in my head, I felt the same excitement that I had on the real hunt. I stopped. In the cut-over. It had happened there. Somehow I knew that when the hounds crossed the road into State Line Church there was a hound missing. What had happened? The answer was in the cut-over.

The scene came into focus. There had been a house in those woods. Long since burned down. The chimney the only remnant. But no. It was not the only remnant. There had been a well. A hand dug well. Four feet across. Covered with old rotten two by sixes. The well was next to the chimney in a pitiful little clearing—all that was left of some young couple's hopes and dreams of making it on that hard Carolina ground. Or maybe they had moved on to better things, leaving behind the little house to rot and then burn. Leaving just the chimney and the well.

And my bitch was in that well!

Wells like that were almost always dry. But how the hell deep was it? I'd never looked into one. I left the parking lot in a roar. Got as close as I could to the old house site, ran the rest of the way, and out of breath threw myself down on the ground, and could see where one of the old timbers had fallen in. I pulled myself to the edge. Looked down.

And there, 30 feet below, was Roxanne. Smiling up at me, saying either that she had known all along I would come, or saying why did it take so long. Or maybe being just a hound, happy to see her master. I suppose I spoke to her because she made an attempt to climb but really knew it was fruitless. This would take some doing. But she wasn't hurt.

I lay there feeling happy out of all proportion to the situation. She had been lost, and I had found her. I had caused her to come into the world, and she in her ultimate dependence waited—literally waited—for me to come and get her. I wondered if that was how a shepherd feels when he finds a lost sheep.

Suddenly I felt centered again.

I got help. We got her out. She was fine.

Late that afternoon I went back to the clearing with some thick boards to close off the well again. The winter light was failing. As I came into the open, to the house site, I felt a chill—of more than cold. And felt like an intruder. And thought again of the young couple I had created in my mind's eye, and wondered whether they had felt the same chill on winter evenings and felt like intruders. And thought they probably had. And maybe they had an old potlicker hound which the young man took to a meet of his friends on a Saturday night. And listened the night through till dawn came and the hounds' voices stopped, and it was time for home and the cares of the world.

Yes, maybe that was how it had been. And as I fixed the old well cover, the chill passed. I was happy with the story I had made, and felt less like an intruder, and wondered if sometime way in the future someone else would come to this old dug well and wonder and make up a story with me in it. With the hounds running and the land in grass with lots of cows. And the story would have a happy ending with me going back to check the hounds—all there—and then going home to my own clearing with the smoke rising up just right from my own chimney, and my wife waiting.

ᚠ

Lost Hound

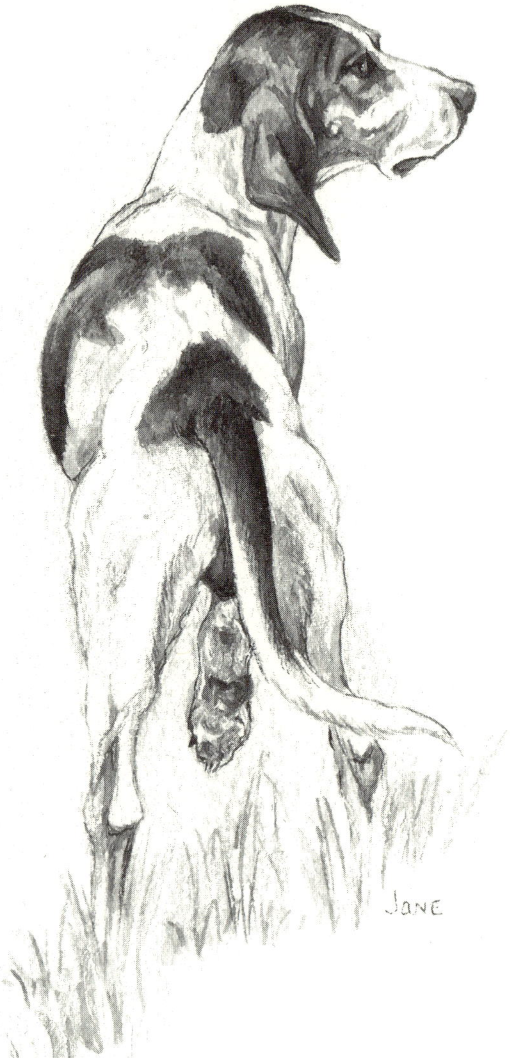
JANE

Lost Hound

If you've ever walked the interstate
You know the dream of summer thunder with
No rain and heat in solemn surge like fate
Gone out of sync—where eighteen-wheelers brew
Their shouted, tire-born songs with diesel breath;
And fast food wrappers feed the session's mood.

And standing on the bank, the hunting horn
A feeble blast in that ensemble, you too
Would wonder why the hound would choose to scorn
The woods' cool anodyne and come each day
To stand head up and staring, stern tucked low,
And set to shun the road crew's charity.

Waiting, it would seem, for me—although
Each time I came too late, and he
Had gone without track or trace to show
The way in grass—until by chance I tried
The other edge and saw fresh prints,
In barren clay, cut straight across the field.

Two weeks lost and now the eye is drawn
To track like rock to sudden earth, and breath
Is short, while still the voice insists upon
Its calling: "Roper, come!"—until a crawl
And certain hitch of skin confounds the mind,
And turning, there he was—in bones and flesh

Drawn taut in hunger's pull, circling down
The wind to prove the ear's uneasy truce with fear.
And when I crouched and called his name again,
He came to catch my hand's unchanging scent;
And in that moment's hush his eyes came clear,
As if to make a mirror for my face.

Dixie

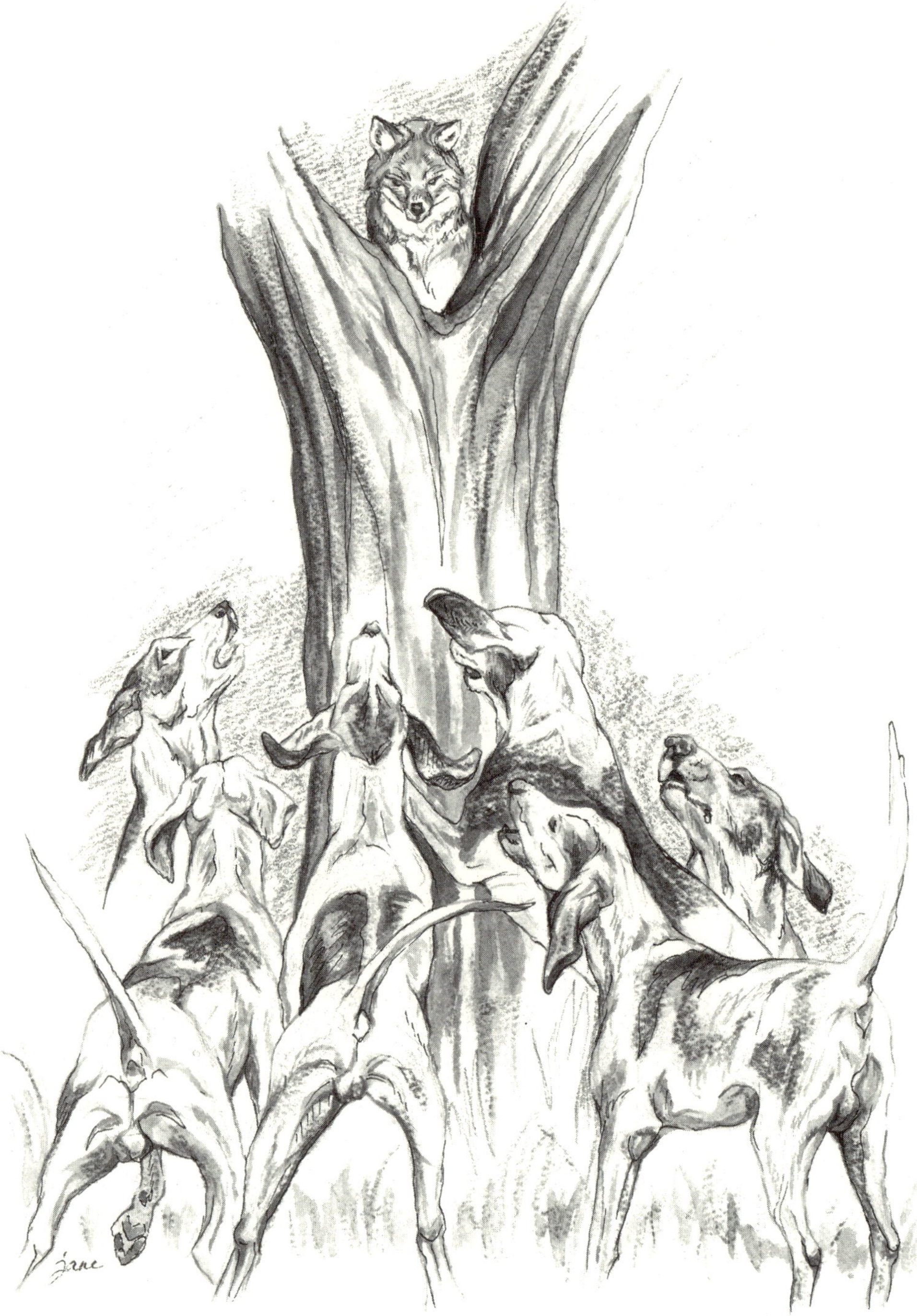

As do most parents, my parents had very specific expectations of me. In my case they were: College. Graduate school. An academic career. Learned Papers. Stay out of trouble. Do what is expected. Etc.

So it is no wonder they exhibited signs of anxiety when, at the end of my freshman year in college, I began spending all my time with horses during the summer, and going foxhunting during winter vacations. Definitely not in the game plan. There was no support from home for that foolishness. So I groomed and exercised to get horses to ride. As a kid, I had cowboyed around the countryside on an evil pony, and had sometimes followed along behind the hunt. I had stopped lessons when I was ten. But folks were generous, and I managed to find mounts to go foxhunting over Thanksgiving and Christmas.

I loved the pageantry, and watching the hounds when they jumped from the truck. But once the mash in the woods started, and you had to look out for your knees on trees, or getting yourself kicked, I wasn't so sure. Paradoxically, when the hunt got going, you didn't see much. But something drew me on—kept me coming back. And then, Thanksgiving of my sophomore year, I met Dixie.

Lost Hound

For some reason, long forgotten, I didn't get my usual horse for the Thanksgiving Day hunt. I was told to get the mare in the third stall on the right. It wasn't a very fancy barn, so you had to duck when you went in the stalls.

I ducked and looked up. The first part of her I saw was her rump. She had a large red bow tied in her tail. She was bay, the blah kind. Long in the back and skinny. She had long hair. A big head. Really long pasterns. In short, I thought I had moved down at least two pegs from my former mount. But beggars can't be choosers. So I tacked up, and we started the 5-mile hack to the meet. My initial impressions were encouraging. She didn't jig the whole time the way my other mount did. And I was told that she only kicked if someone ran into her.

The fixture was on the sweeping lawn of a huge brick house with white columns. There must have been a hundred horses. And lots of scarlet coats and ladies in shadbellies. It was, as they used to say, a brave sight. It looked almost medieval. Yes, maybe that was it. Medieval.

The hounds were cast, and we moved off to the pine woods behind the farm of the long-time huntsman, who had just retired. He was out that day. Riding in the field. A stoutly impressive man in scarlet who sat his Thoroughbred horse with an ease I could only admire and hope that one day I would achieve.

The hunt started. It seemed as if hounds were running every which way. The field reversing. The narrow trails slippery from the light rain of the night before. I tried to look in front and in back at the same time. In front to keep from crashing into the next horse who might kick even though there was no ribbon in his tail. And behind to warn anyone who was not sufficiently impressed with the red bow in Dixie's tail. The pines were full of gullies and little hills. It was an up-and-down place. Usually it frightened me.

But not this time. I was not frantically pulling on the reins to keep Dixie from plowing into the horse ahead, wondering if she would fall down in the next turn because she was on the wrong lead. No, she was just cantering along. No hurry. She knew her place.

Dixie

That day Dixie led me into a different world. A world where I was free to look around as she galloped through the woods, to see individual trees, not just a mass of dangerous green. Free to listen. To strain my ears for the sound of the hounds' voices. Even to watch the antics of the rest of the field, as people dealt with the problems of making it in that huge group of horses. Look! There are some hounds running through the woods with their noses on the ground—mute, looking for the others. And there was the old huntsman, sitting cool on his big horse with the reins flapping, easing through those woods like he was in an open field.

And then we came to a little ravine. I braced myself and took up the reins in anticipation of a headlong charge as Dixie chased her balance down the hill, with me hanging onto her mouth for dear life. But it didn't happen. The weight in my hands stayed as if she were on level ground—and so did her backbone. To a non-rider it would probably sound stupid. So what if her backbone stayed level? But we know different. We know that balance is the measure of a field hunter. That balance is to throw the reins away and have the horse seem to rise in front of you as she carries you down the incline with no change in pace, just level.

There was a fork ahead. When the old huntsman got to it, he bore off to the right, followed by three of his half-wild ponies ridden by kids who looked like urchins in hand-me-down riding clothes. But they were not losing a step to that big Thoroughbred horse.

The ponies could whiz around turns wide open, while the big horse had to slow down, at least a little. The field in front of me followed the field master to the left.

I had discovered in my short time on a real hunting horse that if you gripped with your knees and began a turn in your mind, the horse would do it. And change leads. Never mind why. It just happened. So when the fork came up, without any hesitation or consideration of etiquette, I made a turn in my mind and followed the old man and the wild ponies up the right fork. I kicked Dixie hard to catch up. And when the horse and the ponies checked, we saw six hounds crossing from right to left in front of us

Lost Hound

in full cry. Skinny, with a lot of white. Tails half-naked from beating through briars. The voices sounded hysterical—screaming that if they didn't catch what was in front of them, they would go crazy. Dixie's ears pricked forward, and I felt her stiffen under me. And then we were going again. Flat out. Around a turn to the left, the mare changing leads with no thought from me. Then on, snaking along the narrow trails. She stood up in the turns. That is, she didn't lean over like a motorcycle and make me feel like her feet were about to go out from under her. The scrub pines went by in a blur, but I had no fear of a tree wreck and a ruined knee. Just stayed in the middle of that rocking gait and let her carry me wherever we ended up. All I had to do was duck the mud flung back by the ponies.

One part of me was busy being in awe of that horse while the other was tuned in to our hunt, which circled the entire pine woods, cutting through trails I'd never been on before. Who cared? The old man and the wild ponies were ahead—and just ahead of them were the hounds, their backwoods American voices straining beyond all reason. I could see it unfold. It was like being in a movie and watching it at the same time. Or like a waking dream at dawn when for a time you can write the story of your dream while it is happening.

Sometimes time stops in a situation like that—and you think the run will last forever.

We pulled up in a little clearing, and it was silent. The hounds were at a loss, milling around. The old man spoke to them, and they raised their heads and looked at him. And suddenly he was the center, with the six hounds and the three urchins and me, waiting for him to do something, to show us the way out of this dilemma. Still there was silence.

In the middle of the clearing there was a cedar tree. And unlike most of the cedars in those woods, it was perfectly shaped—like a Christmas tree. Slowly the old man raised his hunting whip and pointed.

A gray fox was looking out from under the cedar limbs, twenty feet above the ground. The red guard hairs around his muzzle swept back along his snout and his eyes were shining. Ears pricked. In that instant he must

Dixie

have taken our measure—of that we can be sure. And suddenly my mind reached out and formed a question for him—the question I still ask, even across all these 35 or better years:

Who are you? Tell me your name.

Then one of the hounds viewed the fox and all hell broke loose. The hounds were frantically trying to climb the tree. The old man yelled for the urchins to give me their ponies and get hold of the hounds. Because behind us we could hear the main hunt running hard, coming back to us. The kids handed me their reins. They grabbed at the hounds and finally the melee sorted itself out. Hanging on like death to two hounds apiece, the boys pulled the hounds to the edge of the clearing. The cry of the main pack became greater and greater until the old man hollered, "Hark!" The urchins let go. And now mute, our hounds tore off to regain the main pack. And it was over—though for me it had just begun.

Were they "our hounds"? Who knows? Maybe for that little time they were ours, mine and the old man's, and the three little boys'. Maybe.

But certain facts remain. The pines are gone. There are houses there now. I never rode Dixie again. But from then on when I rode a bad one, I knew they weren't all bad, that there were Dixies in the world. But she was my first good one, and for that she has always been close in my mind: the bay mare with the long hair and the ribbon in her tail and the backbone which stayed level going downhill. In balance.

And what of the hounds? The crazy, skinny little hounds who hit the ground running when they jumped from the truck. Hounds with names like Spec and Blue and Lonesome. Hounds whose world had little contact with ours. Who would as soon run a deer as a fox. But hounds, who, when once tied to the hot track and hot themselves, gave forth the pure essence of the chase. You wouldn't want any of them, but once heard, their cry would stay in your dreams forever.

And the fox? That, of course, is the crux of it all. What of the fox?

Do you see him standing on the hill next to the single huge oak—a pale flame resting from having easily foiled your hounds at their own game? Do

Lost Hound

you see him at the end of a run where the hounds made no mistakes and are gaining on him, until, at the top of the broomsage hill, in the January wind, he heads for the big earth? And you feel your breath go slack in relief.

And then—standing at the den, cheering as the hounds dig in the timeless ritual of "gone to ground"—you see again that Thanksgiving fox looking out at you from the cedar tree with shining eyes, the fox which you have pursued across all these thirty-five or better years. And you ask:

Who are you? Tell me your name.

ᚠ

How Wild Are Your Foxes?

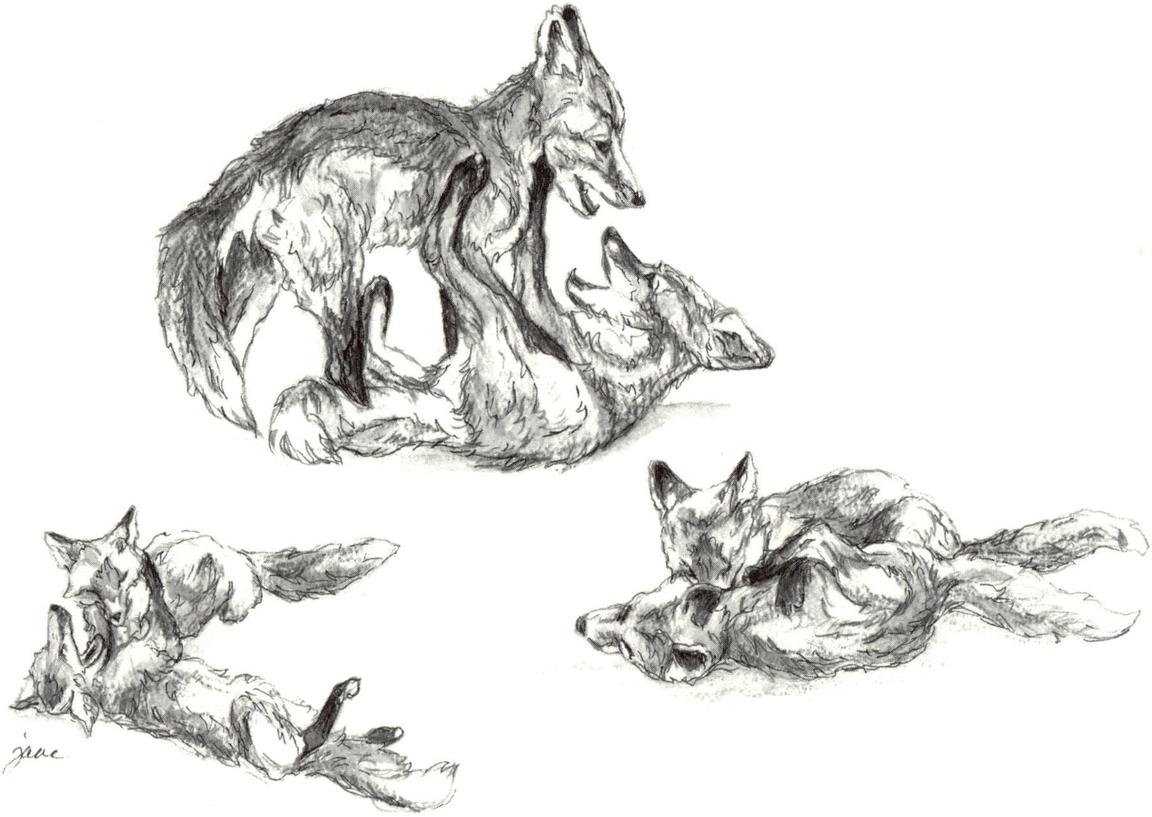

Some people can't resist getting involved with wildlife. If you are among that group, watching foxes grow up can be especially satisfying. The best time for it is in late spring and early summer. The den you choose should be somewhat in the open for ease of viewing. In addition, you must be able to arrive at your vantage point unseen; and you must be downwind. What happens next varies.

One year I had two convenient dens to watch. The first was in the Christopher bottom, which was a flat, triangular piece of land of about eight acres, surrounded on two sides by a creek and a river, and on the third by a hill. Because it was not fenced and too small to crop, it had been let to grow up in weeds the whole previous year. In the early spring, the owner decided to "clean it up." Fortunately, the big, batwinged mower was high enough off the ground that it cleared the mounds of the den.

Two days after the bushhogging a friend found me at lunch and gave me the news. The den beneath the weeds was in use, and she had ridden by it two days in a row and seen the cubs each day. The little ones had glanced at the horse, but kept on playing. It is curious that quite often both adult foxes and cubs will tolerate people going by on horseback, or even on a tractor.

The following day I went over early in the morning and sat on the creek bank, which was 30 yards away from the den and usually downwind. The cubs were out playing when I got there. They were leaping into the air and landing with the stiff-legged pounce they would use to catch small rodents. The trajectory of the leap was natural to them—they were born knowing how to do it. They would become solitary hunters and needed little socialization. By August they would be on their own.

Just as I arrived the second day, I saw the vixen emerge from some honeysuckle at the base of the hill, and hop up on a log to look the situation over, sitting with her brush wrapped tight around her. After a few minutes, she jumped down and wandered over to the den, stood on the mound, and let the little ones nurse.

This scene repeated itself over the next few days in various combinations. By the end of the fifth or sixth day, however, two new things had been added. First, on two days, I saw the dog fox. Each time he was lying at the other end of the bottom in a patch of broomsage, watching.

And I realized that the vixen knew I was there. The first time she looked at me, she was standing on the mound of the den, nursing her cubs. I was startled, for a fact. It was as if on a solitary walk in the woods you turned around and saw someone watching you. The watcher became the watched. I expected her to run, and when she didn't, I felt myself staring back at her. And suddenly the scene was like a photograph, with her in the center, in sharp focus, while the rest blurred, and faded away.

By this stage, the foxes had become a local tourist attraction. Everyone was told not to say a word about them because they would be disturbed by too many people going by. Naturally, the horseback traffic past the den at eleven in the morning quadrupled, at least. And the foxes obliged. The little ones played around the mound for their audience, and even the mother was seen occasionally.

I was sure she would move, so my project had to be done in a hurry. Both the dog fox and the vixen made trips to the hidden place in that area where I put out the chickens, so I knew they were eating chicken somewhere. The question was where. At that time of year, red foxes are supposed to bring home things for the cubs to eat. They are also supposed to have a mess of feathers, bones, rodent skeletons, and other stuff around the dens. The western North Carolina foxes, however, did none of these things. The dens were clean, and not just a few of them—all of them. This was not supposed to be. Hence my experiment.

The first day, I would drive around the bottom, circle the den, and leave—to get them used to the jeep. The next day, if the foxes were still there, I would take a chicken with me and, as I passed the den, I would heave the chicken out the window, drive off, get to my place, and settle down to see what would happen.

It worked. And on the second day when I got to my observation post, the chicken was walking around the area looking for insects and going "Bwaak." The cubs came out of the den and stared at her. I waited. Two or three minutes went by, and the vixen materialized from under her log, looked around, and trotted toward the den, cool as could be. I glanced over at the broomsage patch, and sure enough, there was the dog fox sitting up and watching. When she was three or so feet from the chicken, the vixen stopped. The chicken raised her head, the fox shot through the air, and that, as we say, was the hunt.

However, the vixen did not, as you would have thought, proceed to dismember the chicken and show the cubs what to do. She glanced at the dog fox's position and then mine, turned and trotted back to the log and, as foxes are able to do, disappeared. And then, here came the dog fox, trotting right along. He picked up the chicken and started back to his place.

Do you remember the line from "The Fox" song where, after his invasion of the hen/duck house, the fox "throwed the duck across his back"? Well, there it was: the fox trotting away with the hen, head held high and turned to the side like a puppy pulling a trophy sweat shirt—holding it up so he won't trip on it. It looked exactly as if the fox was carrying the chicken on his back.

The following morning I didn't see the foxes, but I was in a hurry and didn't stay long. The next day when the foxes didn't appear, I knew the vixen had moved. So I made a survey of the bottom. The whole area was covered with a crisscross of little paths. One of them led straight from the den to the pile of chicken feathers, and in fact a number of trails led to piles of chicken feathers, none closer to the main den entrance than 30 yards. It turned out that usually feather piles were even farther from dens in that country, but the creek and river made a natural barrier which required the foxes to eat closer to home.

Of itself, it would have been a most satisfactory fox-watching season. However, it didn't end there, because, while I was watching the foxes in the Christopher bottom, I was also able to follow a litter growing up on Stateline Church hill. Unlike the Christopher den, which was a made-over groundhog hole, the one on the hill was an ancient complex with six or so entrances which had been used by foxes off and on for years.

The approach was such that the best time to watch was in the late afternoon; but by the time I took up the vigil, the parents had begun to leave in the afternoon to hunt, and the cubs were tagging along as well. So instead of going to the den, I tried to intercept the group at some point in their daily rounds. This proved difficult because, by June, the fox family was already breaking up. The daddy might not even show up, and the vixen usually trotted purposefully off on her rounds while the cubs got sidetracked on insects. One afternoon I arrived just in time to see the whole family spread out across the hillside.

What I was interested in was how closely and for how long the cubs would follow the routes of the adults. I knew a place at a game trail crossing where there was usually fox hair on the bottom strand of wire fence. When I removed the hair and it was there again the next day, I figured I was on the right track, as it were.

At first I didn't have much luck. I was coming at the wrong time of day, and each time I changed the time, I was still wrong. Until one afternoon, as I pulled around the stump pile on the farm track on the way to my vantage point, I looked up to see two of the cubs not 40 yards in front of me, trotting head to tail up the path toward my wire crossing. It was freaky, but they didn't see me. I slammed on the brakes, and they still didn't see me.

How Wild Are Your Foxes?

There was a stiff breeze and fortunately I was downwind of them, and of course that is what made it work. Just before they got to the fence, one veered off to the right and made a leap for a grasshopper. The other went hunting—nose down and intent. Suddenly the hunter leapt into the air, made his arc, and came up with a vole clenched in his teeth. The swagger and strut of that fox could have been nothing other than pride.

Head held high, he trotted in my direction. There was a new round bale nearly in his path, and without hesitation he jumped up on it and stood for a second, like a miniature lion.

The wiggling of the vole in his mouth brought him back to earth. He put his head down and let it go, grabbing it just before it jumped off the bale. Next, he threw it up in the air and caught it—which was pretty impressive. And did it again—even more impressive.

Certainly the fox was impressed with himself, because the third time he threw the vole so high that it was obvious to me that it was not going to come down within reach. It was not obvious to him, however—and he made a mighty leap, realizing at the last second he was not only not going to catch the vole, but, more importantly, that he was not even going to come down on the bale. Looking down, he went rigid in the air, his legs spraddled out like a cat being dumped into a washtub (if you have ever seen such a thing).

By the time he hit the ground, he had almost gotten his legs back underneath him, so it wasn't a complete belly flop. Still, it was pretty undignified, and pride entered the picture again. He jumped up and looked around him, and the temptation to say he was embarrassed is overwhelming. On the other hand, you might say that when he hit the ground and came to his senses, he looked around, in fear, to be sure that danger had not crept up unannounced. Or, knowing what you do of vulnerability, you might say that the two are part of the same thing, and isn't it interesting how connected we all are?

ᚠ

The Old Hen in Fall

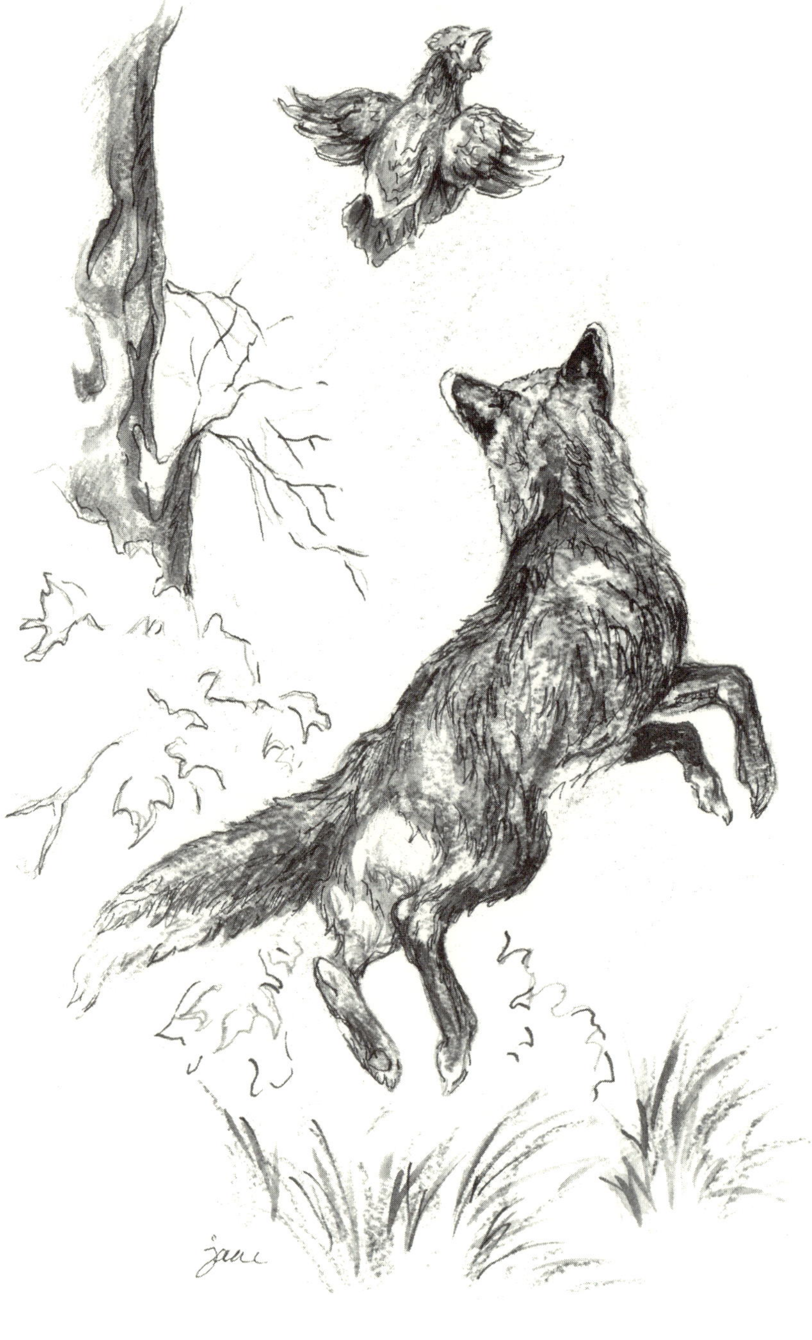
jane

The Old Hen in Fall

Above her naked neck the old hen's head
Bobbed and jerked among the dying weeds,
As rusty yellow eyes sought the wood
hawk's sliding shadow—though until that hour
The laying shed's mechanic world had worked
Its will upon her life with faceless power:

Watered through a tube; fed by a chain;
Sun subsumed in the electric timer's whine;
Her glands arranged for economic gain.
Until they stopped from age—or spite—and I,
The huntsman, paid the salvage fee. The signs
Were clear: her battered comb was pale and dry.

I bought two hundred hens (the price was right)
And put them in my pen, and took a few
That day, in autumn's slanting yellow light,
To feed the foxes, and in one place stopped to watch
As crows in curious outrage shrieked and drew
The fox awake from beneath a tree stump's crotch.

Lost Hound

He trotted to the weed field's edge and stretched,
And heard the Wood Hawk's whistle as she skimmed
The failing trees, her tilting shadow etched
In autumn light, careening down the hill.
The fox, the hawk, the hen, the scene was caught
In brownish-red and suddenly gone still.

Of course a trick of memory stills that scene.
That flight could not be stopped. Nor could the fox's
Furious plunge across the paling green
To seem, beneath the shadow's final fall,
To merge into the old hen's heaving wings,
A wild embrace which stilled that whistled call.

ᚠ

Why Hounds Hunt

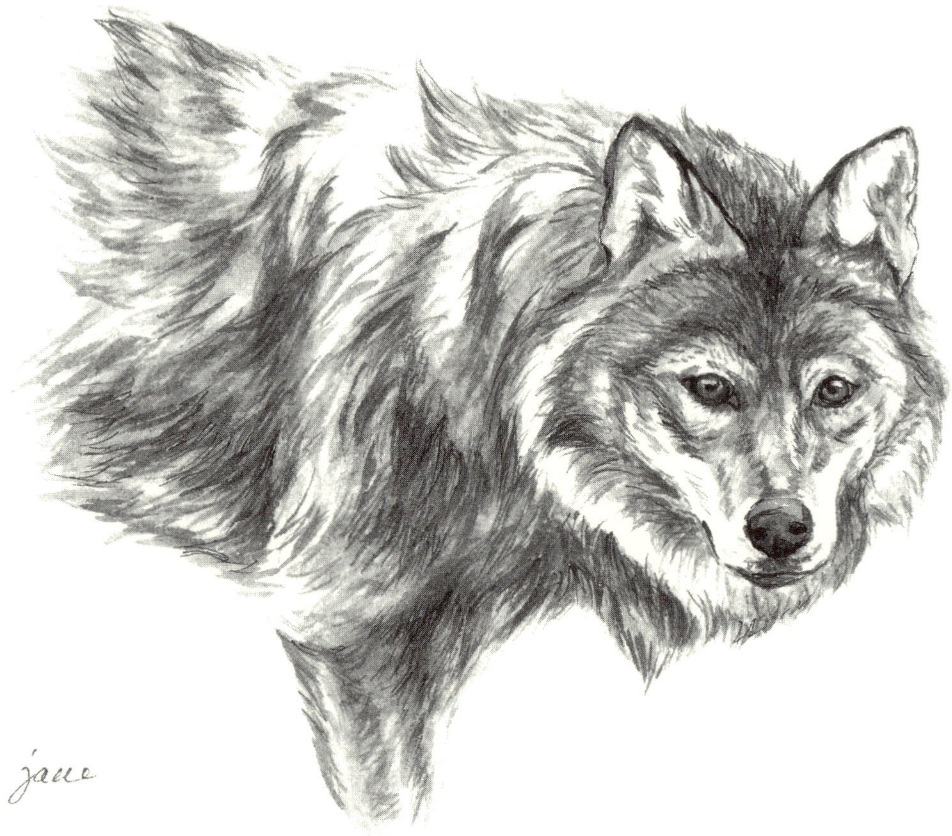
jane

A perennial topic for discussion among foxhunters is the question of why hounds hunt and run quarry when they so seldom (at least in North America) catch it. After all, for the hounds, the chase is the instinctive reenactment of their method of living: the organized pursuit of food. So why, if they are to keep doing it time after time and day after day, should it not be necessary for them to have the reward of capturing and eating their prey? In England a very different situation exists with regard to catching the fox. Many British foxhunters will assert that for a pack to be at their best, they must have the reward of catching their quarry.

However, the American experience of the chase—of both foxhunters on horseback in the day and endless numbers of night hunters—would seem to belay the Britishers' point. Too many of us have listened to packs completely unused to catching the fox run in full cry for extended periods of time. And further, if the fox has crossed a dangerous road and the hounds must be stopped, they do it so obligingly that it seems amazing that one minute they could be in full cry and the next minute, after some whip cracking and scolding, standing, panting, they look up at the huntsman as if to say, "OK, boss, what's next?"

There have been many explanations advanced. One is the notion that the huntsman, by acting as the "Alpha" to the pack is capable, through his cheering and encouragement, of eliciting the hunting response without the reward at the end. The idea is that the dog's world is so rigidly hierarchical that the hounds do it to please their leader. This does not explain why so many hounds have run at night at top performance with no boss at all—just the fox, the night, and the other hounds. An explanation for this might be that, because individually owned night hounds tend to compete, to have a "race," the competition supplies the incentive.

But some of us have the sneaking suspicion that the hounds do it because it gives them pleasure or even joy. They are a little like my neighbor who all his life barely scratched out a living from the hard, red soil. When asked in his seventieth year why he still did it, he replied, "Because I likes it."

So there it lay, at least with me, for many years. The idea needed evidence. And as time went on and research on wolves became available to the general public, evidence began to emerge.

First, the hound, as are all dogs, is descended from the wolf and retains, in a diluted form, his social structure. The most notable point of contact between the wolf's world and hound's is the organization of the wolf hunting unit. The pack is an extended family, consisting of an alpha male and female and various other offspring and relatives, depending on circumstances. This group, which varies in size from about six to sixteen, is organized vertically: the alphas at the top, and so on down to the current year's puppies. During the late spring and summer, the burden upon the adults to supply food for the rapidly growing puppies is very great. The adults leave a "baby sitter" wolf home with the puppies and go off to hunt the prey necessary to keep themselves and their offspring alive, and, in the case of the puppies, growing.

In the Arctic, the main prey is musk ox, a prehistoric looking creature that ekes out a living from the tundra grasses and sedges. The musk ox is a very formidable opponent, however, and the wolves' hunting success is never ensured. They have been observed testing group after group before attempting to kill, and most of the attempts end in frustration. A National Geographic video has been made about wolves which includes sequences of them in pursuit of musk ox. Their testing of the prey has a game-like quality to it, even considering the deadly seriousness of the situation. They often seem to make a feint at a musk ox for the fun of it, without hope of success, as if "practicing" their skills. At other times they pause in the desultory "chase" to take a short nap, and the musk oxen resume grazing. In short, they seem to enjoy the whole proceeding, in spite of the fact that their lives and the lives of their offspring depend upon the ultimate success of their efforts.

I've not seen statistics on success rates in the Arctic, but the eminent wolf biologist Dr. L. David Mech supplies some interesting data for us from his studies of the wolf packs on the Isle Royale, a 210-square-mile island in northern Lake Superior. Over a number of winters he observed from aircraft a large pack of wolves pursue moose. A summary is as follows:

> Of 131 moose that I watched the large Isle Royale pack detect, usually by odor rather than by sight or tracking, 11 discovered the wolves first and left; 120 did not. Of those, 24 stood their ground and fought the wolves when first encountered; the wolves then always gave up the attempt within five minutes of skirmishing and the moose remained safe. Some 96 moose fled, however, when the wolves approached, and 43 escaped before the wolves caught up. The wolves did catch up with 53 and of those, 12 stood and fought, and they escaped. Forty-one moose continued to run when the wolves caught up, and of those 34 outran or outlasted the wolves and also escaped. However, 7 of the moose that ran were attacked, and 6 of them were killed; only one escaped after being wounded. (L.D. Mech, 1988, *The Arctic Wolf: Living with the Pack*, Voyageur Press, Minnesota)

This sample is limited to a prey species which is surely the most formidable for a wolf pack to pursue. But it is clear that the outstanding feature of the summary is the wolves' determination to keep trying in the face of terrible odds.

Behavior patterns like the skirmishing with the musk ox and the pursuit of the moose only occur in an animal's repertoire when they have survival value. And the persistence and the "fun" of the chase seem to fall into that category. The success rate for a wolf pack hunting large prey is so low that in order to keep doing it day after day, year in and year out, they must derive some pleasure from the chase itself. The wolves' close-knit social and family structure also enhances the cooperation necessary for the hunting endeavor. But finally, the wolves seem to do it almost for its own sake—because it is "what they do."

Hounds are, of course, domesticated. They have been bred for a very long time for certain qualities: scenting ability; cooperation (as seen in the close bonds of the wolf family); and the "will" to keep trying in the worst conditions, among others. They are bred almost exactly in the evolutionary niche of their ancestor, the wolf; and hunting is "what they do," also. But because their hunting does not have the deadly seriousness of the wolves, it is possible for them to have what I shall call the "joy of the chase": that quality which makes them take such pleasure in the hunt itself, successful or not.

After a bit of research on wolves in the wild, there can be little doubt where these hunting qualities in the hound have come from; because, for both the hound and the wolf, the journey would appear to have become as important as the destination, for how else could they cope with the frustration of hunts ending with no quarry?

And so we are brought back to the words of my neighbor; and this time we hear the voices of the hound and the wolf added to his. And when asked the question, they reply together, "because I likes it."

ᚠ

Fluter

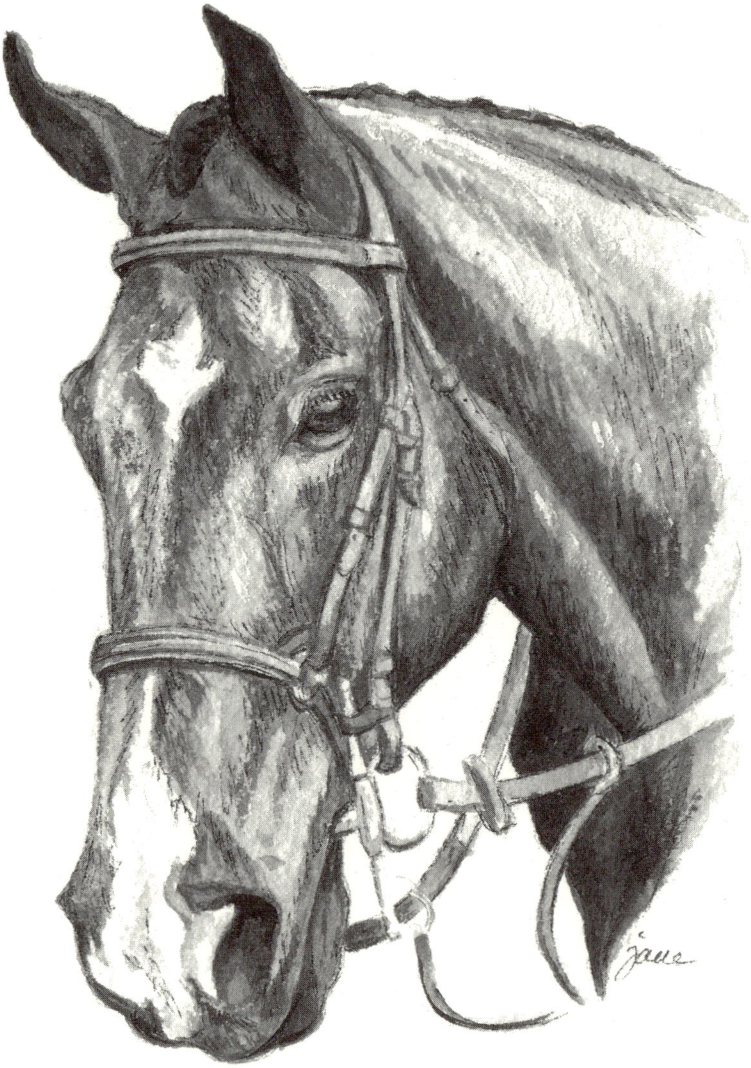

When you are twenty-three, and your wife is pregnant, and you are making $4,500 (a year) teaching English in a boys' prep school, and living in an apartment in a strange city, and have no cash money, the last thing you should do is buy a horse. You especially shouldn't buy a Thoroughbred 5-year-old gelding in an advanced state of emaciation with a serious injury to a front foot.

We had been in Kansas City for 6 months. Joe Mackey's legendary riding stable had welcomed us with open arms; we were even given a subscription to the Mission Valley Hunt, because the Secretary of the hunt was also Secretary of the board of the school where I taught. I drove the truck to the hunt meets, and for that we had free mounts. And because we had colors from a Virginia hunt and were therefore assumed to be experts, I was asked to whip-in, despite the fact that at the time my total experience as a hunt staff member consisted of laying the last drag in the history of the Farmington hunt and riding along with the huntsman one morning when all the regulars were sick.

What I lacked in experience and knowledge I more than made up for in enthusiasm: because by then I had fallen to the pull of the hounds' voices; and the smell of the countryside on August mornings; and the roar of joy when the pack strikes a hot track deep within a cornfield.

Lost Hound

One Sunday evening during that first winter in Kansas City, Joe's barn manager, Claude Coons, called to say that I had better get out there quick because there was a horse that I needed to buy, and one of the girls who rode at the stable was about to…. The idea was absurd.

He was a bay, 16 hands and had tall withers, made taller by how skinny he was. And a big head. And a neck which seemed barely adequate to hold the head and withers together.

And dark, kind eyes. Interested, but a bit reserved. Eyes which conveyed that certain quality which a friend once called "knowing, and then knowing."

And flop ears. Which he pricked when he came down to a nasty fence or got aimed at a huge gully. Most horses who prick their ears are frightened and liable to stop. There were many times over the years when he must have been apprehensive. Maybe even frightened. But he never stopped. He just wanted to be sure of what he was getting into. We called it courage.

And the injury. Probably a wire cut which nearly tore the inside quarter of his right front foot off, causing it to contract into a kind of mule foot with the inside wall nearly vertical and always difficult to get a nail into. I can't remember whether he was lame that day or not. Given the overall picture, it didn't make much difference.

Obviously it was a wasted trip…. "Get the tack," Claude said. Why? The horse is nearly dead of starvation. He insisted. Colorfully—as was his style. So I got the tack and got on him.

The horse had never seen a fence before. He cantered around the ring in perfect balance. He trotted over cavaletti. Then we put a little oxer after the cavaletti. The oxer got bigger and bigger. Three foot six, square. Then we shortened the distance. From the beginning he raised his knees exactly to the right level, bent his pasterns, hocks straight up, and went over the fences rounded.

Claude stood in the center of the ring, grinning.

I am not taciturn by nature. By the time half an hour of this had gone by, I was so excited I thought I might have a heart attack. You see, even though I wasn't afraid, I was not a good rider. I was too anxious in front of a fence. I had a tendency to take over and then make a mistake. I was not graceful on a horse. And I was very aware of it. From the beginning, he gave me balance.

I bought him for $325 which I borrowed from my life insurance policy (and for some reason, never paid back).

His name was Brushjumper (although Joe Mackey, for as long as we were there, called him "Brushpumper" to everyone's disgust). Even though Brushjumper was an awful name, I refused to give him a "show name," holding vaguely to the biblical notion that names were not to be monkeyed with by mortals. Nicknames were fine. He started off as "Skinny" for obvious reasons. A year or so later my brother, who spent many hours on the basics with the horse, began to call him "Flute" and then "Fluter," which stuck for the rest of his life, with later variations such as "Uncle Fluter." A friend in New England called him "Fluke" which of course he was. Toward the end we often called him "Pop."

There was concern in some quarters that as he got healthy, his personality would change. It never did; he only got physically strong. After 3 weeks of schooling, I cleaned him up, and we made our skin and bones debut in the hunting field. Do you know how you turn up your nose if someone comes out with a horse which looks like a killer? That's what happened at the meet that day. But by the end of the hunt, people were staring at him, and not because he was skinny. This horse was different. This was his first hunt. He cantered down a rocky hill, across a big ditch and then crossed a 2-foot deep river as if he had been doing it forever. Same with the panels. They were little, but he had only been jumping for 3 weeks. He lined up for the jumps. No fussing.

But there was the injury to his foot. A year went by. We dealt with it as best we could. Shoeing. Bute. Finally the vet and I decided to X-ray it. It was awful. The whole inside wing of the coffin bone was broken off. Bill sent the radiographs to Kansas State. The word came back to nerve him. That was the only way. How long would he last? Maybe a year and a half. We did it standing up in the vet's garage. Twenty-three years later, we buried him.

Lost Hound

It is now time to fast forward and hit the high spots. Otherwise it would be a book.

The spring after we got him, I went to help pack-train puppies. Some of them were pretty wild. I discovered that Fluter would watch for a puppy to break free from the pack. Then he would get me into a position to chase the puppy back. Instantly! He must have been used to cut cattle, although that was the only thing we ever did with him which he would not tolerate. Normally he paid little attention to cows. But if you got the notion to herd them somewhere, he would start to sweat and fuss, and lunge out through the air like a maniac. With puppies he was fine.

His reputation made mine. He could do anything with hounds. Over the years he made me feel like no country on earth could stop us when hounds were running. There were times when I deluded myself into thinking that I was doing something more than showing the way.

We sometimes hunted at a farm in Drexel, Mo. One day I was the whip in front—standing in the woods when hounds broke into full cry maybe half a mile away. We were facing the direction the hounds were coming from. Suddenly, Fluter's flop ears went forward. A coyote trotted toward us, and jumped up on a rock, facing us, with one ear backed to hear the pursuit. The coyote looked at Fluter and me and we looked at him. The horse's ears set the coyote at ease. I exhaled. Fluter was the connection.

After a stint in New England with a little pack of our own and Susie winning a big trophy on Fluter at the New England Hunter Trials, among other adventures, we moved home to Virginia.

Our children were eight and ten. Both had ridden Fluter from a young age; and while my daughter, Susan, had always shinnied up the horse's front leg, using his knee as a foothold, Robert usually got on by jumping from the top of a fence to the horse's back, even if the gulf between them was quite wide. The halter was the only tack. Robert referred to these rides as "being run away with." In reality, they consisted of Fluter trotting up and down the fence, refusing to canter no matter how much kicking Robert did.

That particular morning Robert reached up and grabbed the halter to steer with, and got Fluter to go a little way into the field. A few moments later, we turned in amazement to see Robert standing up on Fluter's hindquarters, peeing off his stern, while the old horse remained motionless, as if to insure that the little boy would not lose his balance. It would have been the ultimate Norman Rockwell painting.

A year or so later we were at the Hunt Club during a show. There was a little ring next to the kennel, and jumpers were schooling. There were a couple of refusals. I was watching, holding Fluter. My daughter, Susan, at the time eleven, was standing beside me. The oxer had two bars—the first one 3 feet, then 4 feet to the second bar at nearly 5 feet...Can you do that, Susan? Sure, Dad. Up she went while I made the lead rope into reins. By the time she got to the edge of the ring, I was having vapors over the idiocy of the situation. She started across at the fence. Kick him, I yelled. She did. He met the fence on a medium stride and did his thing, while we all stared, goggle-eyed. It didn't matter how many times you saw Fluter do things like that. There was always a little disbelief.

In the spring of 1975 we were asked to represent Farmington in the Virginia Field Hunter Championships, to be hosted by the Warrenton Hunt and led by Betty Oare. I had never even seen one of the events—let alone been in one. So I did what I always did when I got into a hunting thing that I didn't know anything about: I called Albert Poe, long-time northern Virginia huntsman. Albert is a careful and detailed teacher, so you have to listen patiently to get the whole message. What follows is just the gist of it: On the first part, go in front to show what you can do; on the second, go in back to show that your horse has manners; and then, at the beginning of the third part, start in the back and just let the horse gallop past the whole field and end up in front. The whip cracking and hold hard and gate closing would be a breeze. That is exactly what we did, and Fluter won it. In the fall, when we led the championship at Farmington, the judge remarked to one of the stewards that it was a shame that Fluter couldn't win it twice in a row.

Then came his halcyon days. I served as field-master for Farmington for three seasons. The first year we served he was twenty-one. We all called him Uncle Fluter by then. At a check he had a pose which he struck. Head down, ears a little forward—interested, but not impressed, having been there so many times before. And then would come the hounds' cry, and the swing of his old head as he turned to look, ears cocked. The fox was the hounds' pilot, but Fluter was ours—mine and the field's.

We moved. For me to take the position as huntsman (and later, Joint-Master) in western North Carolina. I assumed that when it came time to road puppies that August, he would be with me. It would be his nineteenth hunting season. I never stopped to imagine hunting without him.

The first day we drew cover, hounds struck a cold track and booed along on it. Pop (as I sometimes called him) flopped his ears, ready to go, once again.

As we cantered across a little pasture, something happened. Suddenly he was breathing funny and his heart was thudding. I pulled up and jumped off. And knew in that instant that it was over.

I talked to the vet about it. But I had made up my mind. As a kind of retirement ceremony—although none of the local people knew him, and some thought it a lot of fuss over an old, sway-backed horse—I rode him to parade the hounds at the fall horse show that year.

I rode him once more after that. We were living at the Cotton Patch. The horses got out one night and trotted up the dark country road toward the village. Susie and I went after them. I had a rope shank along and rode Fluter home bareback. It had been over a year since I had been on him. He was feeling a little spooked by the dark and the occasional car and the strange place. He had his head up and ears forward. There was such power in his step even then, and such awareness in his carriage, that the reality of the situation came over me like a flood: I had to stop looking for another Fluter. Because there weren't any more Fluters.

He lived to be twenty-nine. When I arrived at home one August afternoon in 1988, I heard him whinnying. An urgent, high-pitched whinny. I found him lying in the shed behind the barn. He was sweating. I got him up and held his head in my arms for a moment until he stopped whinnying. His ears were back. I gave him a shot for pain, and called the vet. Four hours later, we put him down.

Fluter

We buried him beneath his favorite cedar tree. Where, during those last summers, he would be standing in the morning when I came out to go to the kennel—dozing, ears a little bit forward. Serene. I had a grave stone cut for him, and the line beneath his name and dates reads:

"EARTH, RECEIVE AN HONORED GUEST."

The line is from W.H. Auden's eulogy for William Butler Yeats.

ᚠ

The Land

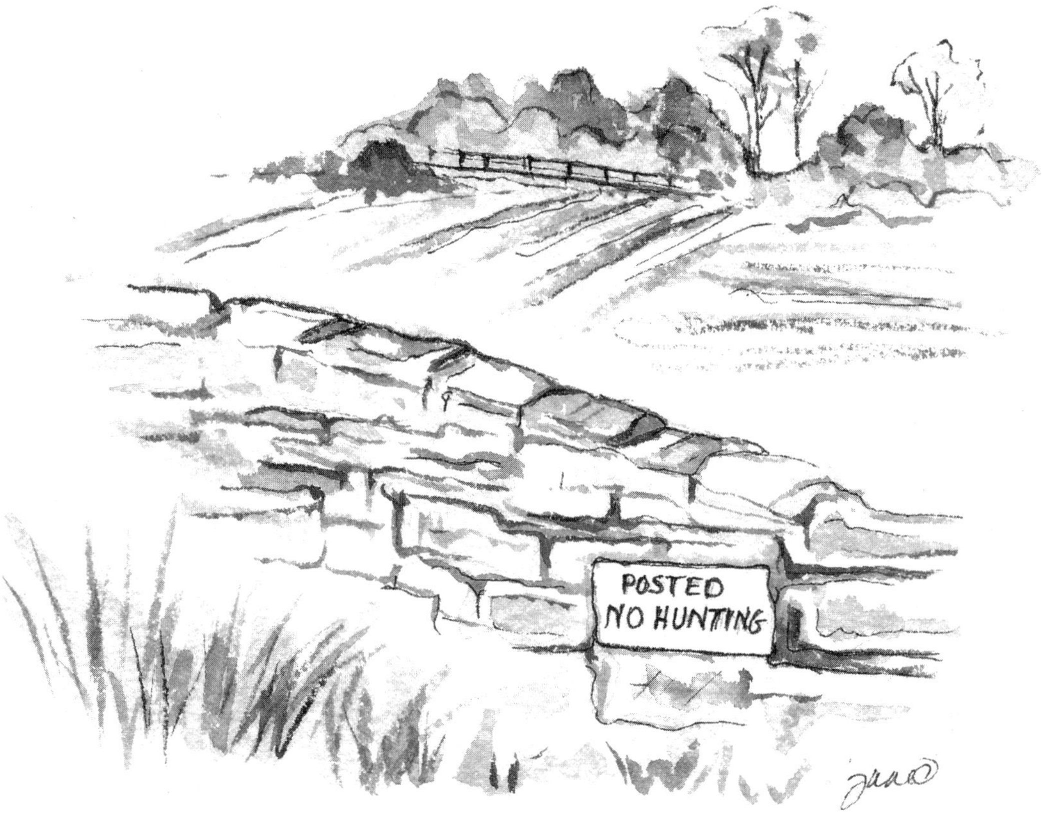
POSTED
NO HUNTING

Curiously enough, I was most often asked by men…Why do you do it? With your education…background…etc., etc. The implication, though seldom with any irony, was, why didn't I get a real job, like other men? In the beginning—nonplused, I garbled something about…I no longer know what. I was never good at that sort of question, particularly in a cocktail party setting.

But as time went on, I developed some answers, though oblique at best. My answers were nearly always questions: "Why are you here? What could have possessed you to move all the way from Manhattan to western North Carolina? There really isn't anything to do here except play golf and go fox-hunting. Are you going to learn to ride?—Yes, I know your wife is interested in dressage. How many horses does she keep?—It takes time for an adult beginner to learn to ride, but lots of people do it. At any rate, we are glad you are here, and glad you bought the 200 acres across from the McCue's." (And here, with a face-stretching smile) "It will be all right for the hunt to come through, won't it?" It was August. We were excited about the new season.

"Oh sure. Don't worry about a thing. Sally and I are going to take a picnic lunch out there on Saturday and post the whole place. No one will be allowed on it but the hunt. No problem."

Lost Hound

The man's name was James Cunningham. Until recently a top executive in one of the major publishing houses still headquartered in Manhattan, now semi-retired.

Otis McCue had a face that was seamed like the land he lived on. His granddaddy had come to that county from farther east during the Depression, when the land he had grown up on finally wore out. He (the granddaddy) had worked himself and his wife nearly to death: farming, later growing peaches, helping people build barns when there was money. Whatever it took. He not only survived, he ended up with 300 acres free and clear, after he logged it for the scrub pine being bought by the paper mill in Millersburg. The land came right on through to Otis, because Otis's daddy was the same as his granddaddy: he worked, survived, did what had to be done, passed it on. The only thing he (the daddy) did besides work and go to church was go foxhunting. At night, on foot. Later in a truck. He usually had about fifteen hounds, and Otis's ma said the hounds were like an affliction sent from the Lord for some sin she didn't even remember sinning—what with the dogs baying all night when they weren't out hunting—and wondering when in the world the men would get back, if they were.

When they paved the roads, it all changed. The country started to break up—to the point where the young men stopped believing their fathers' tales about such and such a night, when old Belle had been on the lead for fourteen miles almost straight away. And the fox in fear for his life had finally gone to ground on the back side of Stillwell's sawmill, underneath the sawdust pile where James Miller got bit by the copperhead and nearly died.

No one from Otis's generation kept foxhounds.

Otis kept two bird dogs. Quail weren't around the way they used to be, but you could still rustle up a covey if you knew just where to look.

The Land

Jim Cunningham had the kind of Connecticut upbringing almost guaranteed to produce a cliché Manhattan businessman: Fairfield Country Day; Choate; Williams; Wharton School; Madison Avenue. You can picture him: tall, regular features; off-blond hair, thinning; the right clothes. Growing up, he no doubt would have been what my daughter used to call a hunk. Married the right girl. She had grown up riding at Fairfield, thus the horse connection. Sounds dicey, doesn't it? It wasn't. Through all of it (his upbringing), he stayed human—kept what used to be called the common touch. Music—jazz—he played the bass. Athletics. Handball. Running. He was bone serious about running.

And so it was that one morning over coffee, at age fifty-five, he announced to Sally that he was going to run in the New York Marathon. She must have almost dropped her coffee cup. He did it. Finished. It was a triumph. To celebrate, he and Sally spent the night in the Plaza Hotel. Had dinner in the Oak Room.

He told me later that piled on top of the exhaustion was a kind of almost crazy exhilaration. A sense of freedom. A kind of "Well, if I can do that, I can do anything" feeling. They talked and talked, and no doubt spurred on by the euphoria of the day, all the resentments about their lifestyle came to the surface. Things long left unsaid.

And 6 months later, 700 miles to the south, in western North Carolina, they owned property—a lot of it—in the hunting country I was responsible for. Their residence was in a fashionable neighborhood of horse estates. And 5 miles to the east was the "farm." There was nothing on it but woods and some pasture and an old chimney in the center.

Jim and Sally fell in love with that chimney. It gave them a sense of history. As if they were following in the footsteps of real people. There were lots of burned-out chimneys in the area. And of course, they all had their history. But this one was special for the Cunninghams.

They owned it.

The Sunday after the cocktail party, Jim and Sally went out to the old Ryerson place, the "farm" for them. They walked the land, posting it as they went, then had their picnic. Just the two of them. Jim said that the silence of those woods was like nothing he had ever experienced before. It was almost deafening. And a little unnerving. Where had the world gone?

———•———

What followed was like fate. The minute Jim had said the word "post," I knew we were in for trouble. So I wasn't surprised when Otis blew into the kennel in his Dodge Dakota on Monday morning with the gravel flying. His normally dark and taciturn face was red. His whole body was drawn up into a ball of rage, his over-large hands showed knuckle-white from the sleeves of the denim jacket he always wore on cool mornings.

"Who the hell posted the Ryerson place?" he shouted — really shouted — in my face.

Why me? Why was he shouting at me?

Because whenever anything happened to change things in the country, I might not be behind it, but I sure as hell knew about it because I was the dog man and from Virginia and was therefore a Yankee, because I came from north of the border — the North Carolina border, that is. And didn't I know the old time foxdogs really knew how to hunt and mine were too fat — it usually boiled down to that at some point in the diatribe. All of this delivered in a breathless rush of air that left him speechless.

There was no discussion of the hounds that Monday: Didn't I know that he (Otis) had been bird hunting on the Ryerson place for the last 40 years? And didn't I know that the two best coveys in the country were on that place? And where the hell had *these* Yankees come from? Why hadn't I brought them to meet him? And didn't I know that last year he had taken all that trouble to plant a long row of bi-color lespedeza — to try to help the habitat I was always talking about? And what the hell was I going to do about it? And I better do it pretty damn quick because the season opened pretty soon, and he had just got that young bitch back from the trainer who charged him all that money, because he (Otis) didn't have the time to train her himself. And if he had he would have made a better job of it than some expensive city-person from clear the other side of Charlotte. And if I didn't solve *it*, he would come in here and he would shut his land off from the hunt. Nothing personal, but he'd be damned if any Yankees were going to come in here and shut off ground that his daddy and granddaddy before him had always hunted as well as himself his whole life.

———•———

Otis and I were friends. And once when we found ourselves sitting on a bank in late spring, looking at his corn bottom, arguing mildly about whether the cubs the vixen was raising in the den in the middle of the field would kill the young quail at the Ryerson place, a silence fell between us so hard it was like something you could touch. And we both knew what the silence was. And what it meant. Knew that in the grand scheme of things, it mattered not one jot whether the cubs raised in the middle of that field killed the young quail over on the Ryerson place. But knew that it meant something unspeakably important to us. That that red clay cornfield, terraced by his daddy's mules and worn out raising cotton, was passing out of existence before our very eyes. In a way we mourned that field's passing as if it were alive, as if we could hear it groan under the weight of its own history. A field never very fertile, a field capable only of small yields, but a field drenched with McCue sweat. A field which, if it could have spoken, would have asked, "What now?"

And sitting on that bank in the spring of the year with all its vernal promise, we knew the answer, but could not bear to speak it.

———•———

Otis drew his breath, fists still clenched:
"Is he still down here?"
"Yes, he said he didn't have to go back until Wednesday."
"Bring him by this evening. About six. You heard what I said, didn't you? If I can't hunt that farm, you can't hunt my farm."
Yes, I had heard.

Lost Hound

Jim and Sally were having lunch when I drove in. Sure, Jim would be happy to meet an adjacent landowner. I explained the situation. Jim's face clouded over.

"Well, I own the land. I paid for it. Doesn't he understand that?...Well then what is the problem?...If I let your friend hunt over on our place, I will have to let anyone hunt there and I won't do that. I don't like the idea of a lot of strangers walking over the farm with guns. I don't like guns. The hunt is one thing...."

There was a pause:

"And doesn't your friend realize that some day he will want to sell that land, and that it will be somebody like me who will buy it? Sure I'll think about it. But I don't like *quid pro quo's*. But pick me up at a quarter 'til six."

I took out the chickens that afternoon. And as I stopped at each game crossing and left an old worn-out laying hen, my mood didn't relax as it usually did doing that job. Otis and the Ryerson place were placed in such a way that if I lost either of them, I would be effectively cut off from about 2,000 acres of important country. In that country, that was a lot of land.

What do you do? Neither would listen to the other's stories. What did Otis care about Jim and Sally in that room in the Plaza Hotel talking out their stored-up resentments about the Connecticut commute, and the uneasiness, amounting almost to fear, that 3 weeks at the Vineyard in the summer weren't enough. Enough of what? Who knew?

Or Otis, watching the farms around him being bought up by people whose English he had a hard time understanding. And in a way the fact that Otis and his crew helped build some of the new houses made it worse. As if he were helping at his own loss, at a second funeral of his daddy.

I had been through these meetings before. The native, shuffling his feet, looking at the ground. The Yankee open, straightforward, friendly but usually aware that this was not going well. That something was missing.

The meeting between Jim and Otis was no different. Otis made his

The Land

speech about hunting over the land for all those years. Then Jim made his speech about not liking guns, and if he let one, he'd have to let everyone. And how he wanted to be fair.

On the way home, Jim was upbeat. Why would Otis cut off his nose to spite his face? (For some reason that figure of speech was often used to describe why Otis and his people would see "the light.") Surely he would realize where his self-interest lay.

And then he made again the point about people like himself being the ones who would ride in like knights in shining armor and save the day by buying up the no longer profitable farms.

"He'll come around," Jim said as he got out of my jeep. "He struck me as an intelligent man. He'll come around."

The evening felt like lead as I drove back to Otis's. I pulled into the driveway of the one story brick house without a plan. Not even a thought.

"Well, what the hell did he say? Does he know how to be a neighbor? He looked like a smart man to me. Did he get the message?"

"Otis," I said, "here is what we are going to do. You go ahead and hunt in there—he doesn't spend but 3 days a month down here so far—and Sally won't come around on her own. Just don't say anything to anybody. He'll come around. I'm sure he will sooner or later."

Otis said okay, but it was my responsibility.

I went home and tried to forget about the whole thing. Maybe Otis would be too busy to get in there at all.... There were other things to worry about.

Two weeks went by. On the second Friday evening, the phone rang. Of course it was Jim. Could I come over? Sure.

Jim met me at the door.

"He blackmailed you, didn't he? And you told him he could go in there and hunt. Without my permission." Jim was getting angry. The situation bordered on the unique for him. He was used to being in control.

"Why did you do it? Don't you understand what I could do to you and the hunt?"

I had heard it before. Of course I understood. Better than he could know. But I also understood that when you have nothing to lose, you take your best shot.

I tried to keep my face impassive, but I must have failed, because I suddenly realized that he was looking at me differently, that he was seeing in my face that which I wanted to hide.

"What is this thing that you do, anyway?" he asked. "What difference does it really make? Why do you people care about it so much? You are a grown-up, adult man with a wife and family and a fine education. I thought you were all strange at that first cocktail party. Now I know you are...." His voice trailed off. "Tell me why."

So I tried. And in the end he agreed to let Otis go bird hunting over his place.

It was getting dark as I drove the country road toward home. The mountains come right down to the Piedmont there. One moment it can be light and the next moment the sun is gone and night takes over. The early fall evening was soft.

It had been no victory. It had just put off the day when each one of us—Otis and me and maybe even Jim—while sitting on some bank, somewhere—would have to answer the land's unspoken question. The question we could not bear to answer that day on Otis's bank overlooking the corn bottom:

"What now?"

ᚠ

Old Ronda

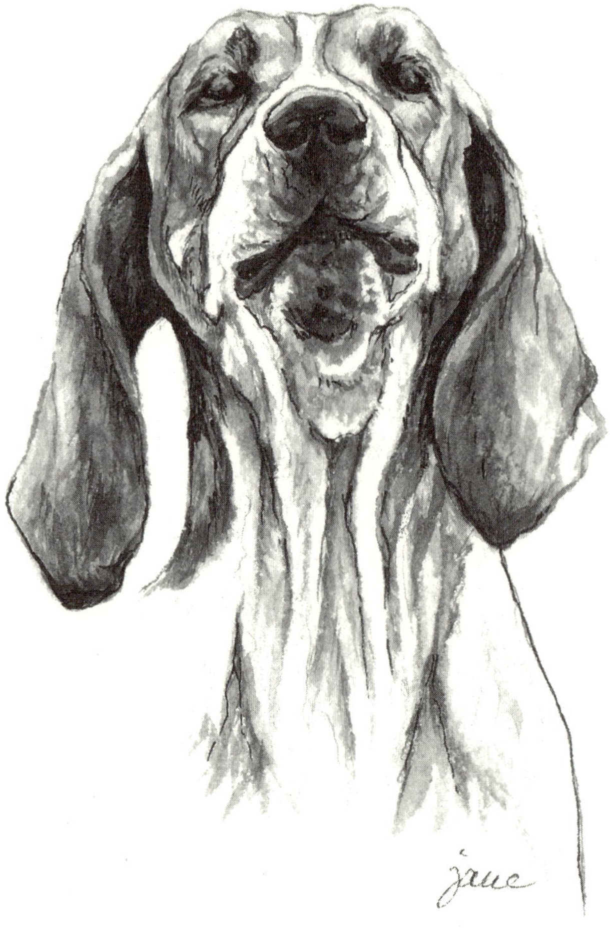
jane

She was one of those wonderful heavy-boned, powerfully built American hounds bred by Albert Poe in the late '60s and early '70s—while he was still huntsman to the Piedmont. She was anything but the light, airy individual some people expect in an American hound. To be picky, however, she was a little long in the back, a little heavy in front, and a bit thick in the neck.

Her head was her most striking feature. Her ears were long and low set, and a hump in the bridge of her nose between her yellow eyes made her look something like a goat.

In years, she was only nine, but those years had been hard ones, and it was obvious that her hunting days were over. Even her lower lids had relaxed and begun to hang down like the eyes of a bloodhound you would see on television. In short, she wasn't a hound you would naturally go wild over and just have to have.

But she did have all the right names in her pedigree. And her litter brother, Norfolk Winthrop, was a popular sire. And it is hard to find the brood bitch of your dreams alive and available. So, because she was both alive and available—and I was about to take a position as a huntsman in North Carolina and would need brood bitches—I took her.

Lost Hound

While we were still in Virginia, she lived in the aisleway of one of our barns, tethered by a light chain. We put a 55-gallon drum on its side for her to get into at night.

After she had been with us for a week or two, we began to let her loose around the farm when we were there. She proceeded to examine all the barns and paddocks in great detail. Her perception of the world was mainly through her nose. When she was busy checking on some arcane smell, it was almost as if her senses of sight and hearing ceased to exist. You could yell at her from 20 feet away and get no response. And in order to make her see you, you had to get right in front of her and intercept her as she worked on her latest olfactory interest. When you did finally get her attention, she would look up, startled, as if to say, "Oh, there you are. Where did you come from? I was busy."

One of the reasons we knew she had a great nose was the volume of air which she sucked into it in the course of her peregrinations. When she was on what for her was a "hot track," you could hear her snuffling a barn length away. And because of her unique powers of concentration you could actually get close enough to see her pulling up dust particles into her nose, prompting the obvious question of why it was that her lungs didn't fill up and suffocate her.

She had reached the stage in her life when she no longer felt compelled to gain ground on whatever she was following. It was as if she could now savor the deliciousness of her scent world without considerations of ambition or competition forcing her forward on the line; however, when she did get started, if you happened to have her on a leash, you had better have taken a good hold, because she was still very strong.

My daughter Susan discovered this most dramatically in the parking lot of a shopping mall. She had taken Ronda for her twice weekly visit to the veterinarian.

Ronda had to visit the vet so frequently because along with her other vagaries, she always seemed to be "sort of" in heat. So we were trying to understand her heat cycle by having her examined twice a week.

Old Ronda

While Ronda was with the "obstetrician," Susan went to Domino's and got a pizza which we had previously ordered, thinking to kill two birds with one stone in one trip. Susan was driving a VW beetle. She picked up the pizza, took it to the VW and laid it on the passenger's seat. Then she went to pick up Ronda. Now, Susan had been around horses and hounds all her life, but her experience had not equipped her to realize that she was approaching the VW from downwind. Suddenly Ronda began to get strong. Susan thought it was nice that Ronda seemed anxious to go home. And wasn't it interesting that Ronda was doing her "snuffling" with her head up—in a parking lot, no less.

Then they reached the car and Susan opened the door. The situation suddenly clarified itself as Ronda made a lunge for the pizza. Being a girl not easily daunted, Susan hauled back on the leash and managed to slam the door. Which saved the pizza for the moment, but presented the problem of how to get Ronda and the pizza home in the same car, especially one the size of a VW beetle. In the end she managed to get the pizza into the front compartment of the beetle and Ronda into the passenger's seat. They arrived at home with Ronda staring out of the windshield like a pointer, as she sniffed away at the pizza, right through the steel dashboard.

Ronda soon expanded her range to include the cottages which surrounded the barns. The farm where we had our Thoroughbred breeding operation was owned by a lady who had converted all the farm buildings except the barns into rental units. She was away much of the year, and we looked after the rentals when she was gone.

Most of our tenants were graduate students from the university. Occasionally, however, we got someone who just wanted to live "in the country"—usually for the first time. One such was a pretty young lady with long blond hair and tender sensibilities. Early on she saw a mare being bred. She watched from her porch in rapt attention as the mare was covered. But when it was over, and she snapped back to the real world, she was appalled and told us exactly why in graphic detail.

She got used to seeing mares covered—but then she bought a dog.

Lost Hound

First, the dog—which was a 3-month old Shepherd—chased a foal. Strangely, after the dog had been screamed at a few times, he stopped chasing foals—and took up chasing cars. I couldn't stand it. There are few things more pitiful and aggravating than a dog trying, in a primordial and atavistic fit, to kill the right front wheel of your car.

I pulled out of the farmyard one morning totally psyched to teach the damned dog a lesson. When he made his dive at the wheel—snarling savagely—I slammed on the brakes and leapt out in avenging fury. I had brought along my hound whip, which I cracked as loud as I could as I yelled at the dog. With a squeal, he headed across the little lawn to his door. And just as he arrived at it, the young lady appeared. She had heard the commotion. But before she could say a word, the dog plunged right through the screen door, into her living room, still squealing.

Two days later the dog left. The screen remained unrepaired, and the young lady just remained.

There was a lake on the farm. It had a big floating dock, and the residents of the farm liked to swim and sunbathe on it. The young lady did, too.

One warm spring afternoon, moments after she had returned from the lake, we heard a blood-curdling yell issue from her cottage. This was not your usual scream. This sounded like something you would hear at a horror movie. Like she had seen a dead body, or something.

Then she emerged from the door at a gallop, pointing back into the cottage—for the moment, speechless. At which point, the object of her horror, Ronda, casually walked through the hole in the screen door, swinging her tail and looking particularly friendly.

After a while, the young lady wound down enough to tell us what had happened. She had taken off her bikini in the bedroom and modestly wrapped a towel around herself for the trip to the shower. And when she pulled back the curtain to turn on the water, there, staring up at her with great solemnity, was Ronda. Startled, the old hound let out her houndy version of a woof. And the girl nearly went into cardiac arrest, fleeing the scene, the towel somehow still clutched about her.

Old Ronda

Now in all fairness, it must be said that if you opened your shower curtain and saw Ronda's head with its goat's eyes staring up at you like a satyr, you might freak out too.

Fairly soon after that, the young lady made other living arrangements. We were all relieved, because she was obviously unhappy with "country" living.

The breeding season was coming to an end. Little by little we started packing for the move. We sold our freezer, and one Saturday morning the purchaser came to get it. Complaining and heaving, we managed to get it out the front door, by taking the door off its hinges, and into the man's truck.

My son Robert, whose appetite for books was as voracious as was Ronda's for the scent world, decided that after all that lifting and heaving, he would spend some time on the couch reading. But yes, he would be over to help on the farm in a while.

Moments later, we heard a sudden shriek of laughter from the house. Robert emerged onto the deck, hollering and laughing and pointing back toward the living room. At the top of his lungs he demanded that we come immediately to the house and see what had happened. We couldn't imagine.

He had been lying there, reading—absorbed—with the outside world tuned out. Suddenly a clicking sound, like fingernails, intruded into his consciousness. Then he heard the snuffling sound which had become famous in the little world of our farm—and raised his head in time to see Ronda come across the room. She had walked right in through the open doorway. As usual, she was navigating by her nose.

Robert later said that she never deviated from her course as she crossed the room and walked straight into the fireplace, which was full of ashes. There was a huge snuffle, and for the only time during her life with us, her lungs filled up. She turned around, faced Robert, sat down in the ashes, and exhaled. Two streams of ashes shot forth from her nostrils—at least ten inches, according to Robert. Thus she became in our family folklore a cross between a satyr and Puff the Magic Dragon.

Lost Hound

None of these experiences left her any the worse for wear. In fact, because of the attention she got, she seemed to become more self-aware. She began to realize that she was pretty cool. And after the move, she loved being in the kennel again.

She eventually had five puppies—we saved three. When the puppies grew into adults, she passed into a more general folklore, for she became known as the dam of Rambler, Regent and Robin. They were handsome hounds, in spite of having a mother with a head like a goat. Hounds who had her nose and all the desire to gain ground on the track, which she must have had when she was in her prime. Hounds who passed these same traits on to their offspring.

ᚠ

Young Ronda

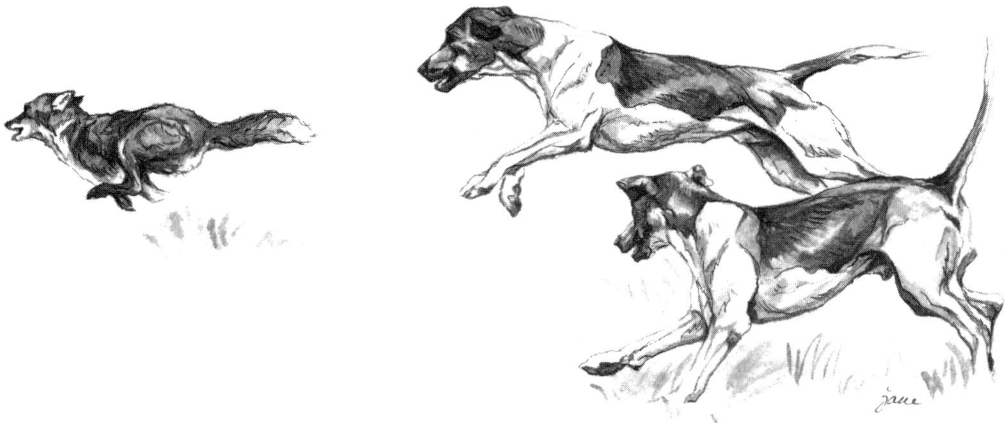
jane

Several years ago our club membership became obsessed with Jack Russell terriers. As a result, we began to have "terrier trials." And after a while we even built, at considerable labor and expense, one of those artificial labyrinths called a "go-to-ground." So intense was the interest in this project that our labyrinth was constructed to International Standards and had an advanced tunnel with two right angle turns, and a novice tunnel, much shorter, with one turn. Where the tunnels intersected, there was a little place with bars so the rats wouldn't get hurt.

This complex was located directly in front of the clubhouse. At the time of construction, one of our newer "associate" members remarked that it certainly would be neat if a fox moved in there. This statement, needless to say, was greeted with good-natured derision by those in the know.

The summer after the go-to-ground was completed, we had a heat wave. Those July mornings—with humidity at a zillion and the temperature edging toward the nineties—were enough to make you stay home. But in spite of the weather, we met each day at the kennel to pack-train puppies and walk out with the older hounds. Adding interest to these sessions were the "night lines" left by nocturnal meanderings of various neighborhood cats. When the younger hounds—and, truth be told, some not so young ones—put their noses down to sniff these "cat tracks," they were soundly rated. But rather than saying, "Ware Riot," or "Have a Care," we said, "Trash!" It somehow sounded more "American."

Each morning when we had finished working with the puppies, one of the whippers-in stayed behind to help me walk out the older hounds. On one occasion, the older hounds were particularly interested in the "cat tracks" in the area of the go-to-ground. We hollered, "Trash!" at them and went on to a place in the shade where they could roll around in the grass. This was always an enjoyable time for me, as I could be sure no one had been hurt during the night, and daydream about all the great runs of the coming season, assuming it ever cooled off. But it was truly hot that day, so we didn't stay long. Again, as we passed the go-to-ground, the hounds wanted to put their heads down. So just for the hell of it, I bent over the little dungeon where the rats were kept during the trials, and started cheering in a shameless manner as the pack crowded around to see (or sniff) what was what.

At which point the whipper-in screamed, "There he goes!" in a tone of voice totally unbecoming a staff member. And as I lifted my head to rate *her*, I viewed the fox streaking across the yard, toward the trees, his white-tipped brush streaming out behind him.

Imagine the scene: the whipper-in in a state of near apoplexy, the hounds grouped around their master and huntsman as he coolly considered the situation; and young Ronda, granddaughter of Piedmont Ronda, who having no scruples about the time of year or dress or humidity or temperature, and knowing that she had just seen a vision, had a 10-foot jump on the rest of us and was already throwing her tongue. (Appropriately, she was also a great-granddaughter of Piedmont Wrestler, who, Albert Poe once remarked to Buster Chadwell, had the loudest voice of any hound he ever bred.)

The fox, having laid up for the day in the advanced tunnel, had finally decided that staying in there while all about you were saying, "Traaaash!" was one thing; but that staying in there while I was hoicking—and the hounds were breathing heavily into the entrance—was quite another.

So, as we say, he split the scene. And after weighing the situation carefully in my mind, I cheered on the whole damn pack.

Young Ronda

Now all your experience to the contrary notwithstanding, I guarantee that seldom in the history of the sport has such a roar issued from the lips of 12 couple of hounds; although, as required by various natural principles, the roar began to grow dim as hounds raced toward Route 14, not quite a mile away.

Clearly, a decision was in order. There were no horses available and the country immediately surrounding the kennel was so thick that a horse would have been of little use anyway. The jeep was next rejected for basically the same reasons. Which left us with the options of either playing night-hunter and waiting for the run to return—should we be so lucky—or following on foot. Now, it is not my nature to be passive, especially where hunting is concerned; and so off we went on foot, with climatic conditions as described above, through dense pine woods replete with bull briars, ground hornets lying in wait, and deer flies so large they would show up on radar.

As we struggled through the dense cover, I heard hounds turn left-handed. I was hoping the fox, which was a cub, would head for home, but I could only guess where home was as the area around the kennel was so grown up in houses, we no longer hunted there. Also, I was expecting scent to fail pretty quickly after the first burst because of the dry condition of the ground. This did not happen. But after about a half a mile paralleling Route 14 he turned again and started back the way he had come.

That run gave new meaning to the clichés about cottony mouth and lungs about to burst. And when the fox turned away from us again for a moment, I began to be afraid for the hounds because of the heat. But he quickly turned back, and after about 10 more minutes, the run abruptly ended.

I was never so glad to be at a loss in my life. We came into the open at the new subdivision road just as ten hounds emerged from the woods on the other side of the road.

All of us sat down on the bank. I had no interest in getting to the end of the run as long as the hounds came to the horn. So as soon as I began to catch my breath, I started blowing and hollering.

The scene was pretty pitiful: two people hardly able to breathe and the ten hounds breathing so hard it looked like their tongues would fall out of their heads. As I blew, the rest straggled in and flopped down on the bank in the shade, except the redoubtable young Ronda, who remained rigidly posed like you would imagine Napoleon or George Washington might stand at the end of a successful battle.

Then we had a casualty. Little Rapture went into convulsions. When it happens, they suddenly go to a different world and leave you behind and helpless, except to hold them. The first time you see it, you think the hound will die. And in that heat you feel a chill, and the taste in your mouth is like lead, as she twitches and moans. And you forget for a moment that she will come back—because they almost always do.

Sitting on the bank with her head in my lap, I kept blowing for the rest. And before long they were all in except Rapture's brother Rapid. Then we heard what sounded like a puppy crying lost, and Rapid came staggering out of the woods like Rip Van Winkle emerging from sleep, a look of utter bliss on his face.

They were all safe, and after a while Rapture recovered as if nothing had happened. So we began to think of starting for home.

Back we went through the bull briars and the barbed wire and the bugs—both of us in cut-offs. Because we were on the gun club property, I blew the horn steadily, lest some unsuspecting marksman lately arrived at the club, finish us off.

At this point in these narratives, it is traditional for the chronicler to give the distance of the point, how far as hounds ran, how long the run lasted, and how it ended. Well, I can't really supply any of this information with any accuracy, except to say that we had 12 couple at the "finding" and 12 couple when we returned, and that about an hour and a half went by from beginning to end.

There is one more thing though.

Ronda is old Ronda now. And when, waiting to move off, or at a check, she gets that look of distance about her, you wonder what she sees. And wonder whether the fox of that day long past has become a search image for her. And whether each time she puts her nose to the hot track,

Young Ronda

and feels her voice growing within her, she sees in her mind's eye her fox, surely hers, shoot out of the advanced tunnel of the go-to-ground, heading for the woods.

ᚠ

Turtle Hound

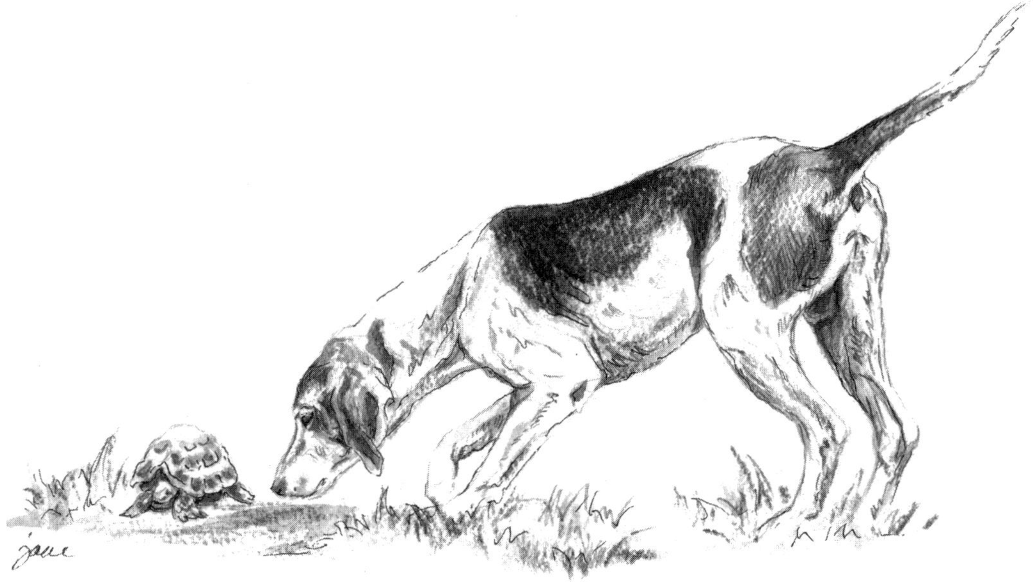

Ready had a lot of distinguished American Foxhound blood in his veins, and as he grew up we all had high hopes for him. He not only was to be a great hunting hound—more important, he was to be the foundation sire of a whole new line. Such hopes are usual among animal breeders (and parents, too, for that matter).

During pack-breaking, Ready showed the usual puppy ecstasy the first couple of times he crunched down on a beer can while walking down the road. But he quickly learned "Leave it!" and let the cans alone. Thankfully—because, clearly, a beer-can-eater would not do.

He had always been a timid little geezer. Not shy in the way of the old-time American hounds, who could skitter between your legs and be gone in the blink of an eye. He was just not very forthcoming. I suppose in all honesty one would have to say that he really didn't have much of a personality. Still, flowing in his veins was the blood of—and all those famous hounds parade before your mind's eye: Piedmont Ronda, little sister to Norfolk Winthrop, and her mother, Robin; Piedmont Rustic, whose sire was Essex Fireman and whose son Piedmont Render appears in every important American pedigree of the last 20 years; Green Spring Valley Poacher who sired a whole dynasty; and the great strike hound, Piedmont

Lost Hound

Charter, who, Albert Poe has said, was the best single hound he's ever bred or hunted—and the list goes on and on. And when you wake up from your reverie, you feel a lot better about your puppy's chances.

Ready made it through the rest of puppy training without a mishap. He learned to get through fences and jump coops and swim the river, as did all the rest of his classmates.

And then came August at dawn; there had been rain all summer and none of the fox cubs had been run over on the roads, at least not so far. The eternal optimism of the first day of cubbing was upon me as I let the pack drift into the covert. There were fourteen puppies that year, and they all went in with the old hounds. They struck a decent track and ran right along, the puppies amazed and excited over the freedom of the thing, and the old ones singing the ageless song of the hunt as if for the first time.

It was a good morning. And so were the next two.

But on the third day, when we finished, Ready was missing. I blew and hollered for him as the rest of the pack rolled around in the grass. No Ready. Five minutes went by, and still no Ready. We would have to go back for him. The field would wait. So I called the hounds, and we started back towards the woods. Just as we reached the edge, I heard the field, behind us, laughing hilariously and turned to where they were pointing.

From the woods emerged Ready, stern waving and head up, with the triumphant demeanor of a puppy with the world's record trophy—a box turtle. He trotted over—growled as the pack sniffed at him—and stood looking up at me like a Lab who has just retrieved the biggest goose in history. The field thought it was a hoot, the other hounds, when they had sniffed the turtle, thought it was weird, and I smiled at him and told him he was good to have found us (even after finding the turtle) while the saying, "Many are called, but few are chosen…" ran through my head.

It's hard to have dark thoughts for long during a good cubbing season. So I quickly remembered the truism that many hounds and racehorses (and children, too) start slowly, and catch up in a hurry when they gain some maturity.

For two times, he was fine. He hunted right with the rest, and ran, too, although not with a lot of verve. He was just along for the ride. Nothing wrong with that. It takes maturity.

The third time we drew through a large open woods. I looked forward to the fixture because I could watch what the puppies were doing and be sure the old hounds didn't get in too much of a hurry. The pack fanned out and began to draw. I noticed Ready out of the corner of my eye, off to the edge, with his nose to the ground.

Then his stern went rigid and began to wave. He jerked my attention right to him. My God, I thought, this puppy is about to strike. He increased his pace a little; and I cast my eyes forward and saw the quarry just as Ready broke into a trot. The turtle was motoring right along, as turtles can, but he shut down in a hurry when Ready picked him up. As before, he was one proud puppy. He was crestfallen when I spoke sharply to him.

The whipper-in riding with me, in the tone of voice which they all use to lay a little guilt on a huntsman, asked, "What are you going to do about him?"

"Nothing," I replied. "He's just immature. That's all. He'll be fine."

There was no way you could beat it out of him—he would just have stopped doing anything.

And so it went the whole first season. Overall, he got better. He even began to hunt a little (for foxes, that is). But there are a lot of turtles in that country (little did I know how many), and when he found one he picked it up. He knew he was not to bring it to me, so he would trot along at the very edge of the pack with the turtle in his mouth. Toward the end of the season, he would even run along with the pack, head down, with the turtle still in his mouth. Once, the field and I watched as he appeared to get so serious about the hunt that he had to give tongue. He dropped the turtle—but then stopped cold and went back for it.

Of course, everyone thought it was the funniest thing they'd ever seen. There was, however, some sympathy for me: "Oh poor him. He had such high hopes for Ready. But that's the way things go (can't you hear the philosophical resignation), and it will be better just to get rid of him, and not worry about it anymore. He just isn't going to make it."

But I kept him. From stubbornness, mainly. Over the summer he filled out and seemed, if such a thing is possible, to grow a little bit of personality. There was just more to him, somehow.

August came and again the season started well, and so did Ready. He got right into the middle of the pack and went to work. During cubbing I think he only picked up a couple of turtles, and those were turtles he happened upon. He had stopped hunting them. But when he did see one, that was usually it. He would try to run, but when it came down to a choice of carrying the turtle or giving tongue, the turtle won.

Late in the fall, having had an excellent season, we had visitors from away. Everyone likes things to go well for visitors, especially the huntsman; and I planned for the first day very carefully. Good things always come in bunches, and sure enough, the hunt started just as I had hoped.

It was a good run until we were at a loss on a little farm road below the leaky dam of a pond. The water from the pond had filled one of the ruts in the road for about 50 yards.

I stood still, thinking: *Let them work it out! They are hyped enough without you getting in there and telling them what to do and maybe being wrong—but damn, we have all those people behind us, and the hounds aren't casting the way they should. And see how warm it has gotten, and the sky is bright blue, and Tripper and Orvis have started looking at me. And there is Ready, trying. At least he doesn't have a turtle.*

No turtle, and 4 months into his second season, he started up the rut, his nose close to the water, stern feathering hard. And when he got to the end of the rut and the water was no longer there, he stopped short. And raised his head and called. With the wonderful note of the true strike hound. Not putting your head to the ground and going on with it before anyone else gets there. No! Calling—saying, "I found it! Come quick and we can all run together!" The hounds honored. And I cheered.

The fox had crossed the river and then eased up in the bottoms, expecting us not to come. Ready had to hunt a little in the sandy soil and then struck again, and off we went. It was as if he owned that fox. Loss for loss you could hear him calling, making it good. At the other end the fox turned and came back and crossed the river again. My horse pulled a shoe, and when they checked the next time, I called them to me. It had been an hour and a half—an hour from where Ready had made his strike. That dog was born that day. I called him, and he came and stood with his front feet on the horse and I praised him. Then I straightened up in the saddle and said to no one in particular, "I told you so," grinning like an idiot.

Of course, the question of the moment was, will he never look at another turtle again? That would have been the romantic thing to have happen. Not the real-world thing, however. Not long after his great day, he picked up a turtle when the hounds were trailing, and I couldn't believe my eyes; however, when they started to run, he dropped the turtle. And then he did it all again: the wonderful calling note when he made good the loss; and the uncanny accuracy of the way he ran the line. Yes, he was going to be just fine.

At the end of the season, we went back to the open woods where, a whole year and a half previous, I had seen him pick up his first turtle. And as the hounds fanned out and began to draw, I watched him. About halfway through the woods, he came upon a turtle, motoring right along, as turtles can. And I stopped on the horse and watched. How could he completely ignore something which had been so important to him—just pass it by without a glance? But he did. And when I called his name, he looked up and I smiled at him, and we went on.

ᚠ

Foxhounds Asleep

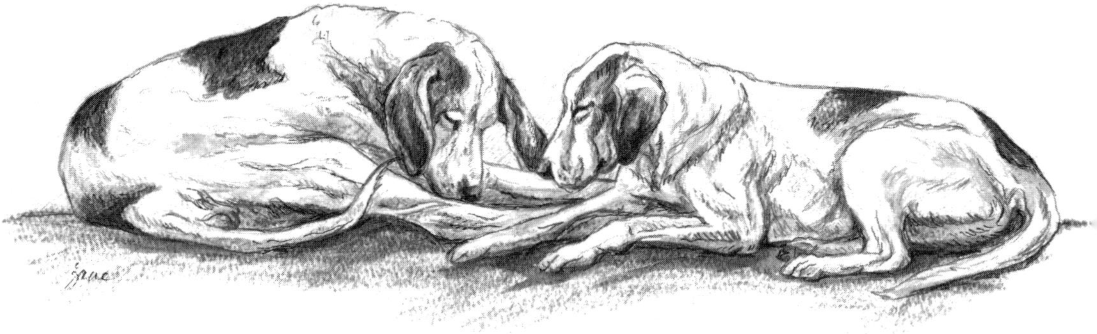

It is thought by some that dog dreams are primordial, atavistic memories of hunting. Others reject this notion as far-fetched, even irrational. Still others cite physiological and psychological factors as explanations of the behavior.

Foxhounds Asleep

While curled about their feet in winter's long
Embrace, two sisters sleep the season's end
And breathe the sunstruck air's elliptic song.
Their sudden cries recall a loss
Where leaves and dust at winter's depth befriend
The fox and stop the voice which sings across

The season's fading track—as if I too
Could share your whimpered dream. And then—
Another dream: the one I watched when you
As deaf and sightless tiny pups, asleep
Beside your mother's fullness, cried aloud
Some ancient chase whose twisted track caught cold

In near mute time makes clear what I have lost.
And yet in August darkness, standing deep
Within the leaves of summer's glut, I've crossed
The moonlit circle cut when water slips
The fox's tongue and seen his image creep
Across the shadowed pool toward the shore.

ᚠ

Mule

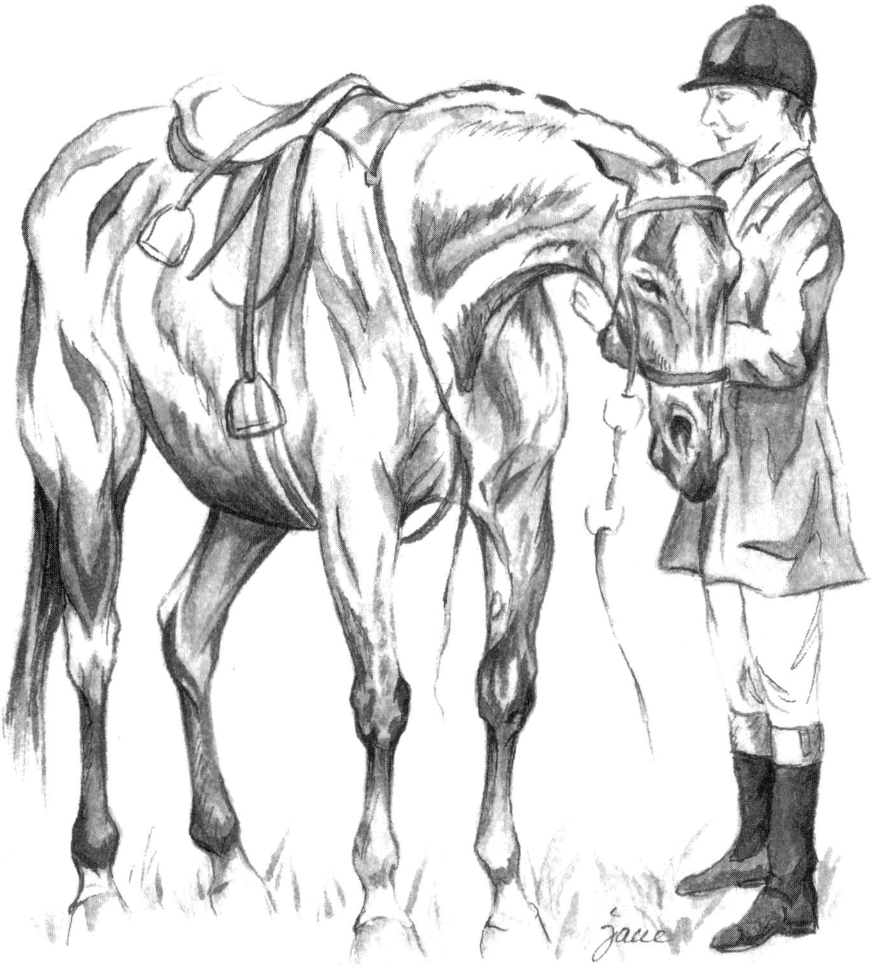

*I*t was a shame to call such a horse Mule, but there you are. As you will see, there was little choice—this in spite of the fact that his dam had been featured on the back cover of *The Blood-Horse*, and the published stud fee for his sire was $25,000. Mule himself was sold at the Keeneland September sale to a prominent owner for $65,000.

In due time Mule was sent to New York, to a trainer as prominent as his owner, to become a racehorse.

But something went wrong from the start, and he finally ended up with me, because for some reason his owner decided that rather than run him cheap and get rid of him, he should find a home as a hunter or a show horse. The owner called one of the salespeople in Maryland, who called my sister-in-law, who called me.

When he arrived, I was thrilled. He really looked the part. He looked like a horse the huntsman in a Munnings painting would ride—with the hounds all gathered around, and the low English sky behind, and the countryside rippling on forever.

The next day I got on him. He shied a lot. Then we went to a creek. Mule took one look at the water, and, instead of stopping short the way most green horses would, he whirled around and took off for home at the gallop. Back to the creek we went. Susie was on her wise staff horse, Posey. At first, Posey stood looking at Mule and me with his usual flop-eared quietness. But as the scene progressed, I swear he cocked his head like a dog as if to say, "What the hell is going on here?"

My feelings exactly. Home I went and got a jockey bat—one of the long, old-fashioned kind.

I lined up for the crossing. I had the bat ready to go. And when he planted his feet, I swung it on him. Hard.

With perfect timing he gave a little buck. Just enough to get me out of the saddle and keep me from really hitting him. When I was out of the saddle, he swapped ends…etc.

We finally got him across. Susie got behind him with the hound whip, and with great precision, cracked it on his hocks just as he stopped dead at the creek. The horse shot out through the air like a Lipizzaner stallion doing airs above the ground. I was glad that I came down in the saddle.

Back and forth. Making a huge leap each time. Never touching the water. Until we said to hell with it. That was enough for one day. One other thing: during this session, I thought I heard him make a funny noise. Not exactly like a windy horse. But weird.

The next day I began his training over fences. In order to get to the schooling area, we had to cross a bridge over a river. The horse refused the bridge. And then we had the same deal as with the creek. Susie came on Posey…etc.

Lest this get boring, I will skip a number of weeks and catch you up at a more advanced stage of Mule's training. He hated barrels. Especially three barrels on their sides with a 4 x 4 on top. His refusal techniques had become more advanced. You came around a turn toward the tiny jump, and as soon as Mule got it on his radar, he would stop—sometimes 50 feet away. Then came the whole routine. Fairly soon it became obvious that something had to give.

I called a friend in Virginia, with whom I had been through some terrible horses. I told him the story.

"Get rid of him!" he said.

There was a long pause…(Ah, vanity thy name is more than woman). I said I didn't want to…yet. What should I do? Grudgingly, he made his recommendation: If I was to continue in this idiocy, I should get some sharp spurs and have it out with him. Either he will learn or go crazy. I had nothing to lose either way.

He learned. Once he realized that his refusal technique had really unpleasant consequences, he got right on with it. It was amazing. He became a good jumper. But he never stopped shying…and he made that little noise.

By this time he had fully earned the name Mule. But how he could run! And that first season I had him was made for it: No drought. Foxes. Country in good shape. And at last the pack was really starting to get it together. It was great.

Toward the end of cubbing we had a hot spell. One Saturday morning in a piece of the country we were about to get subdivided out of, we got into a real fox race. I let Mule ramble down an old logging road to a creek. He still shied at creeks, so I cussed at him from habit, and we ran up the hill into the open.

The hounds had gotten the jump on me, so I got into him as I started across the field.

And then he stopped. I was about to cuss him again, when I felt him wobble a little. Then I realized he wasn't breathing. Not just choked up. This horse was not out of breath: He was not breathing. At all!

I jumped off and yelled to the whipper-in to go on with the hounds. I stood there watching him. And suddenly I went cold inside: he was dying—I was sure of it.

I couldn't stand that horse for all his refusals. But when hounds were running—and he had left his fear behind, and the wind was keen in his nostrils, and the way was clear ahead—he fit into his niche in life like a soft hand in a silken glove. And when that happened, he went to another place and took me with him. And for that it was hard not to love him.

And then—as suddenly as it began—it was over. He did something between a burp and a cough, spit up his soft palate (as I learned later), took a huge breath, and was Mule again. Someone told me a dropped noseband would help.

That night I called the trainer, again. Yes...he did remember that horse had swallowed his soft palate a time or two...no problem. Just put a figure eight noseband on him.

One morning later in the fall we found right off. The fox ran up the river toward the forbidden part of an important farm. There was no normal way to cross the river. There would be no whipper-in there to stop the hounds.

That farm was essential to our hunting. Somehow I had to get to the hounds if the fox crossed the river—which he did. I needed to make a detour—up the river to cross the old bridge, which hadn't even been cleared of kudzu. It looked spooky.

The only way I got across the bridge was to run at it nearly wide open. And by the time I got into the bottom across the river, not a hound was to be heard.

And then, as I looked toward the woods next to the training barn, I saw two old hounds: Orange County Cain and Middleburg Rastus. A season before, they had been the finders. But now the pack had progressed beyond the two old hounds' failing stamina, although they still made it good at a bad loss.

But I let them come along, because they both possessed one of the great hound virtues: they did not give tongue on a covered track. Which meant that when they got left behind, they galloped along the track as best they could—not saying a word, not drawing the puppies from the front or confusing the tail hounds, until, at a particularly bad loss, they caught up, and helped out again.

By the time I caught up with them, they were about 100 yards into the heavily overgrown woods, heading up the hill.

Mule hated branches and bullbriers, and by the time we hit the open field, he was really rattled. And instead of being greeted by the cry of hounds, we were greeted by the roar of Interstate 26. Rastus and Cain crossed the farm road at the edge of the field, heading straight for the Interstate, through cut-over woods from which the logging debris had never been removed—cut-over which had grown back to a height of 10 feet.

My only other encounter with that Interstate had resulted in the death of the fox and the lead hound—with Susie running up and down the median trying to send hounds to me over noise which you have to experience to believe.

It was a musical ensemble from hell: the tenor whining of tires over the bass of the engines' roar. And when I raised the horn to blow, the futility of it came over me like the smell of diesel exhaust. So Rastus and Cain and Mule and I plunged into that thicket, with not a squeak from any hound in front of us.

A dead branch caught the breast plate; it broke and Mule stepped on it and it was gone. Then we found another hound. Rastus and Cain kept on. I brought up the rear with the straggler; Mule stumbled on through the piles of rotting branches on the ground. The roar of the highway got louder. We came to the edge of a wash which was 5 or 6 feet deep and 10 feet across. Mule slid down one side of the wash and collapsed against the other bank, and lay still for a second, his sides heaving. One of the cheek pieces on the bridle had been snagged and broken. He staggered out of the wash, onto a piece of flat, open ground which was covered with moss.

It had been a little clearing in the forest. A clearing where for some reason the loggers had not piled brush. A clearing left exactly as it had been before the loggers came. A refuge in that ruined landscape.

And there were the hounds. Heads up and staring. Sterns tucked. Listening to the roar. I hollered at them, but for a minute they didn't even turn to my voice. Then slowly they seemed to be able to focus on me rather than the noise—which was above us, up the final bank, another 100 yards farther on.

Mule's bridle was a mess. The bit was dangling. The horse was covered with scratches and little cuts. He was shaking from the climb up the bank.

Lost Hound

I got off, undid the bit and hooked the reins through the noseband, remounted and called to the hounds, and we started back.

Mule scrambled up the steep bank to the farm road and stood trembling from the stress of that terrain. But we had made it, and had come away from that place—with the stragglers catching up as I blew for them.

As we started home, Mule walked with his head down. I could feel the rhythm of his exhausted body beneath me, swinging along. We passed a mailbox, and at the very last moment he noticed it, and swerved—too tired to really shy—but unable, even then, even in the grip of that terrible fatigue, to break the pattern. Even after having carried me to the brink of the Interstate to find the hounds—in that little moss-covered clearing.

ᚠ

Cows

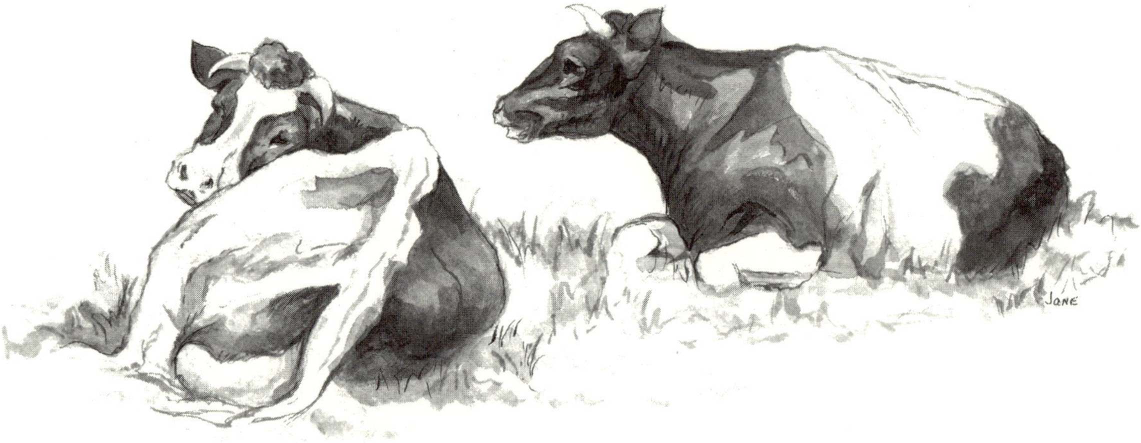
JANE

*I*n a hunting country, cows mean grass, and grass means voles and grasshoppers and other insects and creatures in season, and—if there is clover—rabbits. If the farmers don't have time to cut the honeysuckle and roses which grow up on the fence lines, that's an added bonus. And all these things mean foxes. Cows also mean corn and a great way to start puppies in August. Young foxes hunt the corn fields for rodents, and the puppies and a few old hounds hunt the young foxes in the maze of stalks. No one gets going very fast. The fox twists and turns.

But I digress, for there is more to cows than pasture and fun. Farmers are protective of their cattle, as you might imagine. And when you are opening up new country, problems arise. As you know, cows are either beef or dairy. Beef cows are easy, relatively speaking.

Say a man has a cow/calf beef operation with thirty cows on 100 acres of rough ground. That usually means he has (or more accurately, the cows have) the calves in March. He sells the weanlings in the fall. Unfortunately—though—not before cubbing begins.

And say his 100 acres are right in the middle of a piece of hunting country you are trying to open up. Here is the way the first interview might go: The farmer comes to the door and you exchange pleasantries and your mouth is dry because this is really important—at least to you.

Lost Hound

The conversation is strained. But look at it from his perspective. You are a "stranger" in his country. But he has heard of you. You are the "dog man." The fellow who hunts foxes on horseback, etc., etc. He is polite, because that is the way he was raised up to be—polite, even to strangers. But he knows what's coming. And you can assume that he feels a little like you feel when the Fuller Brush man comes to your door, if such a thing still happens where you live any more.

Only it's worse. Because I don't even have anything to sell. I am trying to get him to let me do something which has the potential to do him harm. Namely, have thirty dogs and forty horses and people run through his pastures just as his calves are getting to weaning time. Surely the hounds will chase his calves.

A kind of primal awareness underlies this feeling. He somehow knows that—when you get right down to it—his cows are the prey and my hounds (and maybe me for that matter) are the predators. And what man in his right mind would invite the fox into his hen yard?

In addition to this, there might also be the problem of folklore. It might be that he remembers as a boy hearing about that other "dog man" whose dogs chased Billy Ryerson's daddy's best cow Bertha (the name is important here—this was not just any old cow, this was Bertha) right through the pasture fence, and across the bottoms toward the river. And how she fell into that deep ditch next to the river because the Johnson grass was so high she couldn't see it (the ditch) coming. And broke her neck. And her just 2 weeks from calving. The memory of the countryside is very long.

Or nearer to home. How those crazy dogs belonging to the fellow before you drove twenty cows right through a brand new five strand high tensile fence. And straight down the hard road to the village, and the police had to come and help round them up. And it just goes to show you—because that fence was guaranteed to hold anything in. But it couldn't hold those cows when the dogs got to running them.

"My hounds won't run cattle or calves," I say. "They are broke to death. If I call, they come. Why don't you ask Billy Jamison down the road. He has seen them hunt right through the middle of the Eliot's big herd and never look at a cow. "

"No," he says, "I reckon I just don't want them on my ground."

The man's name is Jason Searle, and he has a second 100-acre tract he makes hay on. Would he sell some? Might. Three hundred bales? I'll pick it up in the field. At least there is an opening.

And if you really get lucky, one cold morning in late February, as you are driving to the kennel, you will look over into Jason's front pasture and there will be a cow lying in the frost, straining—in trouble. You find Jason and go back with him. She won't get up. But after nearly an hour, dripping with sweat and blood and birth fluid, you get the calf out, and he is alive, and the cow begins her work of nurturing. She looks for all the world like Authumla, the primeval cow in Norse mythology, who licks at the deep northern ice. And when the children of men spring up from it, suckles them, and raises them up.

No matter how many times you have seen it, it is still a miracle. And you and Jason were the only witnesses. There is a kind of bond forged at an event like that. It is almost like a kind of conspiracy.

And the following fall you hunt Jason's farm.

———•———

But what about the hounds? How did you get them to ignore cows and especially calves? I stumbled on my solution by accident.

By the end of that first August I had my puppies pack broken and used to rivers and coops and horses. So I took them with the big hounds to a field full of black cows which belonged to an especially sympathetic landowner.

We started across the field. Remember now, the calves were still on the cows. A puppy named Tripper—who turned out to be one of the best hounds I ever had—suddenly focused on a calf who happened to be running to his mother. Tripper's evolutionary response to "prey" cut in, and

Lost Hound

suddenly he was halfway across the field in hot pursuit of that calf. He (the puppy) didn't know why, but that didn't make any difference. His reaction to the fleeing calf was a lot deeper and older than the pack training I had given him. A lot of screaming and jumping up and down and fury and fear (what if the landowner saw this disgrace and kicked us out, forever?) ensued. I must confess that I participated in some of this panic. It was after all the first group of puppies I had broken in that country. And I was pretty sure I knew a lot about the whole subject, etc., etc.

But back to Tripper. He arrived at the calf just as the calf arrived at his mother. And the mother, without preliminaries, proceeded to stomp that puppy's butt, to put it bluntly. Tripper screamed and ran home to his "mother" (me), and that was the end of that. As I remember, we had a couple of others try it that day. But the first cow wasn't the only mean one in the bunch, and very quickly the puppies were "cow broke."

For all the years following, I never thought my hounds hunted through a field of cows as well as I would have liked. And the reason was that they tended to be looking over their shoulders to be sure a cow wasn't after them. I even had a couple of hounds which wouldn't hack through a field of cows. Two in particular would skirt around the whole pasture, staying close to the fence in case a sudden escape was called for. Helpful visiting whippers-in were known to volunteer to go and get the renegades, and thus demonstrate their skill before a new audience. But by the time I said it wouldn't be necessary, the hounds were back and the point moot. And as related in another story in this collection, "Backfire," I once had a hound so intent on his business that when one of the black cows made a dive at him, he turned and bit the cow on the nose and kept right on going. It was one of those things that you can hardly believe even when you are looking right at it.

———•———

Now take all these incidents, multiply them by ten and you approximate the difficulties which come up with a dairy herd. For starters, a dairy farmer can tell you to the ounce how much milk will be lost if a dairy cow canters five strides, the notion of a dairy cow cantering being preposterous in itself. A dairy cow is a kind of freak of man-made nature: a huge udder with just enough bone and muscle to carry it (the udder) around. Those of us in the beef business are primitive when compared to a dairyman. That man knows his cows one by one and their ancestors, too. And a lot of math about feed ratios and things like that.

———•———

By the second season, it was clear to me that we really needed to hunt a new piece of land with a 200-acre dairy farm right in the middle. (It is amazing to me that these crucial farms always seem to be "right in the middle" and thus essential to the whole project. But there you have it.)

This farm was owned by Mason Freeman, a hale and hearty octogenarian of vast experience and humor, who was blessed with two strong sons. And what is more the two sons planned to stay with the farm—surely a rarity these days. The "boys" were thirty-two and forty when I first met them. They had worked out who did what on the farm. (They tried to explain their system to me once, but it was far too complicated to follow. But it worked.)

And—for real—it was a happy farm.

I met the family early on. I bought hay and straw from them. They were a pleasure to be around. And there were times when a simple truck load of hay would take half a day to get. After all I had to be polite. In reality I loved hearing the old man talk about former days. And the things he had done and seen in the county. Of course it was all colored a nice shade of blue. But memory is self-editing and the meadow across Mary's Branch was somehow always more beautiful in the spring 30 years ago than today. Most of the time I believed his version.

The kitchen in the farmhouse was 25 feet long with the cooking section divided off from the rest by a long counter. On the room side of the counter were three huge plastic-covered recliners facing the largest TV available on the retail market at that time. Each day at 12:30 the two boys and the old man came in for "dinner"—a huge meal cooked up over the course of the morning by their mother and wife. Winter and summer. No matter what the weather. In theory the three men watched the huge TV, which was always turned on. But in reality the old man mostly talked. Because now that he was "retired," he had all the time in the world to travel around the county and keep up with the news. On the local level, he knew everything about everything. His two sons and his wife loved him dearly and were happy to listen to his monologues—not only as an indulgence, but because the old man was very canny. There was always a point to his long speeches and those of us who knew him well got rather caught up—waiting for the punch line.

Well, the day finally came when I had to bite the bullet and open the subject of hunting across their farm. And so at exactly 12:30 on a Thursday, I walked into what had become that familiar kitchen, made my manners, and sat down in the spare chair. Nervous as hell.

Of course all three of them had been waiting a long time for me to get around to the subject. After all, they knew how hunting with hounds worked—it was part of their heritage. Mason's granddaddy had kept hounds—which he hunted at night—but it was still the same. And it was obvious that their farm was important to the new country I was opening up. Yes, they had been waiting.

But there were problems. Real problems. Did I understand? Yes, I understood. The cows could be really strange. And they had the herd mentality. If one acted crazy, they might all act crazy. And some of them were really cranky. And to have that whole herd of forty cows get moving would be awful. Not to mention the heifers. Yes, they knew my hounds wouldn't chase the cows. But....

And what about the horses—the cows had never seen horses.

And there wasn't any fence at all down next to Mary's Branch where the swamp started.

Cows

And what about the people in the field? I couldn't look out for them all the time. And you never could tell about city people who were Yankees to boot.

And even if the cows got used to the whole thing, you had to start somewhere, and what if the cows went crazy and ran through the fence the first time?

"Let me bring some old hounds and two other riders, and we'll just walk around and see what happens."

There was no earthly sensible reason for them to let me do it. But somehow it tweaked their interest. It had been a long time since there had been what they called a fox race on their farm. And, at bottom, they were neighbors and friends and understood how much it meant to me. So they said yes, we could try it.

I swear it was like an audience before the queen. You can't imagine the tension in the three humans. But the hounds were just fine. And although one cow trotted about 20 feet, the trial was judged a success. We continued bringing horses and the hounds until the cows and heifers didn't blink an eye when we came past. We even cantered (the horses, that is) some.

Fall came and we started the new country. Next to the dairy farm was a huge covert of cutover and pine with Mary's Branch running through it. There had been a litter of foxes in there that spring. The parents ate the chickens I brought for them. We had several runs on them that fall. But the fox always headed down the branch toward the swamp. We would gallop along the bottom below the dairy and go into the swamp where the fence was down. Several times the cows were on the hillside overlooking us. But they didn't seem to notice us. I was relieved.

In January we had a Saturday which was a hunting day made in heaven. The morning temperature was in the high thirties. There was no frost in the ground. Air and ground temperature about the same. The overcast was like a ceiling slowly lowering over us. Had it been cold enough, you would have thought it was going to snow. A little breeze was blowing up Mary's Branch, right into our faces. I put the hounds in at the head of the big covert.

Lost Hound

First…trailing. Puppies. Then one old hound. Orvis. Another. Tripper. Then a crash of voices. Here we go. But no. They shut up. Could this be a gray? I'd never seen one in there. Silence. Don't say anything. Let them do it. And then, wham! But he doubled back. Made a full circle around us in the covert. Hounds struggling. Back where he started, and suddenly they were on and going. The whip was already at the foot of the dairy hill. Watching. I was afraid they weren't all together. But yes, there. I could hear them break covert into the field. Pouring it on.

I crossed the branch and galloped down the trail to the coop which gave on the field. I looked up and saw a nightmare about to come to pass. The whole pack, bunched together appeared to be running right at the cows—who were lying out on the hillside. You could see those big old cows chewing their cuds even at that distance. Not for long, though, if that pack ran into them. And just to finish the picture, there was old Mr. Freeman and his two sons, standing at the top of the hill waving their caps wildly. Surely, I thought, waiting for me to do a miracle.

But then, just as the catastrophe was about to occur, the pack veered off down the hill about 150 feet below the cows, heading for the swamp, running wide open.

Not one cow moved. They lay there, chewing. I looked back as we galloped down the hill. The Freemans were still waving their hats, but it looked to me as if they were cheering, also.

The voices of the hounds—aided by the lowering sky—made the swamp ring that day.

On the way in, the whip told me what had happened. She had taken her usual vantage point where she could see but not be seen. The fox was one of the young reds, not a gray. And when he broke cover, he headed straight for the cows. The Freemans were also watching the show. None of the four had ever seen a fox run right at a dairy herd before. But that is what he did. Until he somehow seemed to tune into what was ahead of him. He promptly bore off down the hill, just as the hounds did, as they followed him.

As soon as I had taken care of the hounds, I jumped into the jeep and tore over to the Freeman's. They were milking. The old man was standing in the door of the milking parlor, talking. He had a slow way of talking, occasionally punctuated by a stream of tobacco juice. When he turned to me he smiled:

"Bob (pause), when that fox come out of Ridgley's (pause) and started toward my cows (pause) I thought to myself," and here he started to pick up speed, "…why never in a million years would I have thought that it would be a fox to bother my cows instead of the dogs or the horses. And do you know, when that fox ran past the cows, every single cow in the herd turned her head to watch him go by. And not one of them stopped chewing her cud. I never saw anything like it in my life.

"But then when the dogs come out of the woods, I thought, well, hell, they're going to do it now. The dogs'll miss the track, and that'll be that. I'll have cows everywhere. But they didn't, and the next thing you know, we're all jumping up and down, yelling. It was the damnfoolest thing you ever saw."

He stopped. And that long look of the past came into his eyes. He stood there a moment—not chewing, not moving. Then he turned to me and said in his slow way again:

"Bob, when I was a boy, I used to go with my granddaddy some Saturday nights. The men sat around the fire, listening to the hounds. And talking about which one was on the lead and where the fox would run next. I got so I could pick out the voice of old Blue. She was Granddaddy's favorite. She had a grand voice. And finally I'd curl up by the fire and go to sleep. And wake up at home because Granddaddy picked me up so careful, when it came time to go.

"Yes, I did love to hear the dogs run.…Yours sound good, too. Yes, it is a grand thing to hear…the dogs running."

And then he was motionless again. Caught deep in the grip of his thoughts—in the grip of the past and that faraway sound of a world gone forever. But a world which for him had come alive again that day—with the fox and the hounds and the lowering sky. And the cows—in the reverie of their own deep, self-fulfilling destiny, chewing. Chewing, and the old man and his two strong sons, standing together on the hillside, cheering.

Backfire

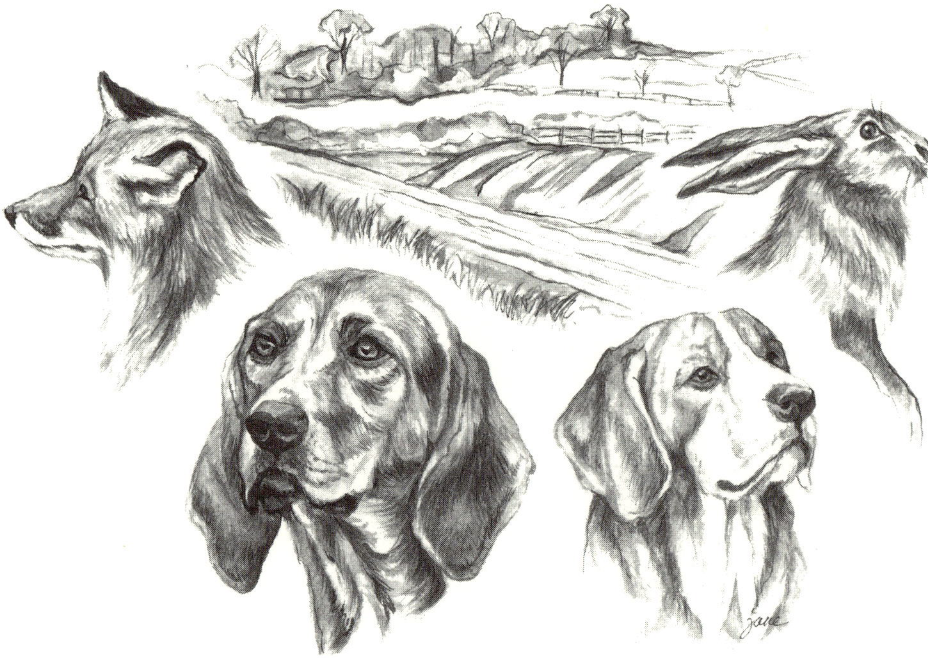

When I took the position as huntsman in western North Carolina, relations between the fox hunting and rabbit hunting communities were strained, to put it mildly.

I was warned about this, but in my innocent arrogance I thought I would be able to take care of the problem in one meeting, or two at the most. However, when I discovered that the rabbit hunters still blamed the foxhunters for a crash in the rabbit population which had occurred more than 30 years ago, it became clear that there was more to it than I had envisioned.

To make matters worse, it was alleged that the crash was caused by the foxhunters putting out spotted rats for the foxes to eat. Eating the rats not only made the foxes fat, but more predatory as well. Hence the rabbit crash.

The problem at that time was that the rabbit hunters felt it should be clear to any thinking person, unless a Yankee—defined as anyone living or having been born north of the North Carolina line—that the foxes ate all the rabbits, thus ruining the rabbit hunting, etc., etc., *a priori*.

A game biologist from the state came to speak about the relationship of predator to prey, how to build brush piles, how to make wildlife borders, and to encourage landowners to sow clover.

Lost Hound

I saw the rabbit hunters; they saw me; we said, "Hello," but that was all.

Every Friday I put out chickens at strategic places for the foxes to eat (no doubt making them more predatory) but what was I to do? In addition to helping the foxes stick around, this activity gave me the opportunity once a week to touch base with the whole country. It was a peaceful, enjoyable chore.

One Friday, late in the fall, I heard the beagles. It was one of those days where the pre-winter clouds are a ceiling over the land, and sound carries like it does in an auditorium. A year before, the landowner clear-cut his woods, giant beeches and all, and across a half-mile of that brutalized landscape the beagles' voices carried to me as if from 50 yards away. Two men stood outlined against the sky, listening. The voices of the little hounds sounded like a boys choir.

The men were on their hill, I on mine, listening. But not for long. The cry faded as the little pack went over the far hill; and I found myself picking my way through the cut-over, trying to get to the next hill to hear what would happen. The tree laps were thick and I hadn't cut a trail there. The men, Clyde and Bryson, had gone out of sight. As I got to the ridge, I heard the hounds picking at the scent. A voice here, a voice there. I hurried. They broke into full cry. Breathing hard, I stopped in a little open place, next to a huge beech stump, looked up, and there they were—Clyde and Bryson—watching me.

I was surprised. I had been thinking about hound voices and trying to catch up with the hunt, not concerned with social and regional problems, but there we were, staring at each other. The situation had to be addressed.

"By God those little boogers are sure talking to that rabbit!"

Silence.

"How the hell do you breed that much voice into them?...How long have you been breeding them?...How many of them are there out there, anyway?"

"Eight."

"Eight? There's no way in God's world that eight hounds could have that much cry! It sounds more like twenty!"

"Eight."

"Well I'll be damned!"

The only sound was those eight beagles driving that rabbit for all they were worth. I looked at Clyde and Bryson, and they looked at me.

Then the dam broke, and we were suddenly just three men with wives and children who should have been attending to the business of the world on a work day. We stood there for a full half hour listening to the hound voices. Then the race was over, and it was time to go. And in the silence of that moment, I felt that most blessed of all hunting feelings: community. And I knew that the sound of hounds' voices would be the bridge across all our differences.

On a dusty Saturday morning two seasons later, I let the hounds out of the trailer so they could walk around and empty while I made polite conversation with a visiting master who was to ride with me that morning. It went something like this:

"Nice hounds. What kind?"

"American. Mostly old Piedmont, but some Essex."

"Hard to handle?"

"No, we work with them."

"Dry!"

"Sure is."

Then I touched the horn, walked to a multiflora rose thicket, and let them drift in. It *was* dry. But I had been watching the litter of foxes raised on the hill behind us all summer. And because I hadn't disturbed them, the young ones were still on their late summer circuit.

It is wonderful when it works; and sure enough, 50 yards down the fence line Ready raised his head and called. Thirteen couple entered and eight couple of puppies answered, and they all went off together across the little creek and into the soybean field on the other side, steadily tonguing the track, while a cloud of dust from the drought raised up over them as they went.

They hit the road and stopped cold. Not a sound. They began to cast up and down the road. The area across the road was part of the cut-over.

Lost Hound

Loblollies had been planted, but that monoculture had been fooled by another monoculture, kudzu, which had reared up like some Old Testament nightmare and killed the loblollies. All that was left was a hillside covered thick with kudzu.

"Will they run through that stuff?" the visitor asked.

I cooled it and innocently said, "I don't know, but we are sure going to find out! Look there!"

At that moment Ready did an unusual thing: trotting down the road he suddenly leapt into the air and gave tongue. It wasn't his long note, I suppose his altitude and time off the ground precluded that, but it was sufficient to the task, because suddenly the whole pack was with him, leaping and tearing through the thicket, down the hill to the next creek. The scent had risen and Ready found it in the air.

"Oh my God!" said the visitor.

The field across the creek was full of mean cows, so we hurried to see if the hounds would be at a loss when the cows chased them.

I jumped the coop into the pasture and yelled for the field to come on.

Then I had heard the beagles ahead of me across the field from the cows, running over the long hill where I had first heard them two seasons before. Loblollies had been planted there, too. But for some reason the kudzu had not killed them. There was a 10- or 12-acre forest; on the far edge I saw the little hounds, about fifteen, dive into the woods, running to beat the band, crossing from left to right in front of me, a quarter-mile away.

And sure enough, the big hounds were at a loss. The Angus cows, even though their calves had been taken off them, were dodging right and left through the pack with their heads down. As one cow came alongside Satchmo, the old hound, aggravated at the interruption of his business, let out a growl and bit the cow on the nose, and then went back to work as she veered off.

I can't remember who found it on the other side, but off they went to the head of the thicket to my right. And then turned sharp left-handed, running hard on what sounded like a collision course with the beagles.

So on my left I had the beagles struggling and screaming their way through the undergrowth, while on my right came the big hounds, their voices sounding abnormally deep in that ensemble. The visitor had his mouth open. The field was lined up right behind us.

Bryson and Clyde and I had discussed the possibility. But we were generally careful to keep the two packs separate. We'd had them running close together, but never like this. Afterwards, it was agreed that they both had always secretly wanted to know what would happen. But being a control person, I was really leery of it.

So there we were, watching, rapt, listening as the two packs got closer and closer. And, in the moment when they intermingled, the cry was like nothing I had ever heard. The range of the voices and the straining and the hounds going two ways at once created an almost unbearable tension. It was like a forest fire of sound: the foxhounds the main fire; the little hounds the backfire, suddenly crashing together.

We waited for the end, but it never came. For some reason, both the fox and the rabbit, like a square dance routine, do-si-doed right past each other and continued on their way. And as the voices separated, and the cry diminished, and the world returned more or less to normal, we cheered, all of us, as Bryson, who had been in there the whole time trying to get a view of the fox, emerged from the pines hollering and waving his hat like a mad man, which is what most people thought we both were anyway.

The runs were wrecked: both the rabbit and the fox disappeared, but it didn't matter. We went on and drew, but it was too dry. And finally we gave it up. The visitor had a good time.

Late that afternoon, I found Clyde and Bryson down at the dusty road where Ready had made his leap that morning. They were standing next to the beech stump where we had stood that afternoon those 2 years ago. And even though we had that amazing run in the same country that morning, the beagles were once again going like hammers of hell. Rabbits of endless energy lived there.

Lost Hound

We just smiled and stood listening—for almost a full half hour. And when the race was over, we all exhaled and started to talk. But the silence had been good, too. Because the hounds' song was our song. And it required no words. It was the bridge.

ᚠ

The Cat and the Swimming Pool

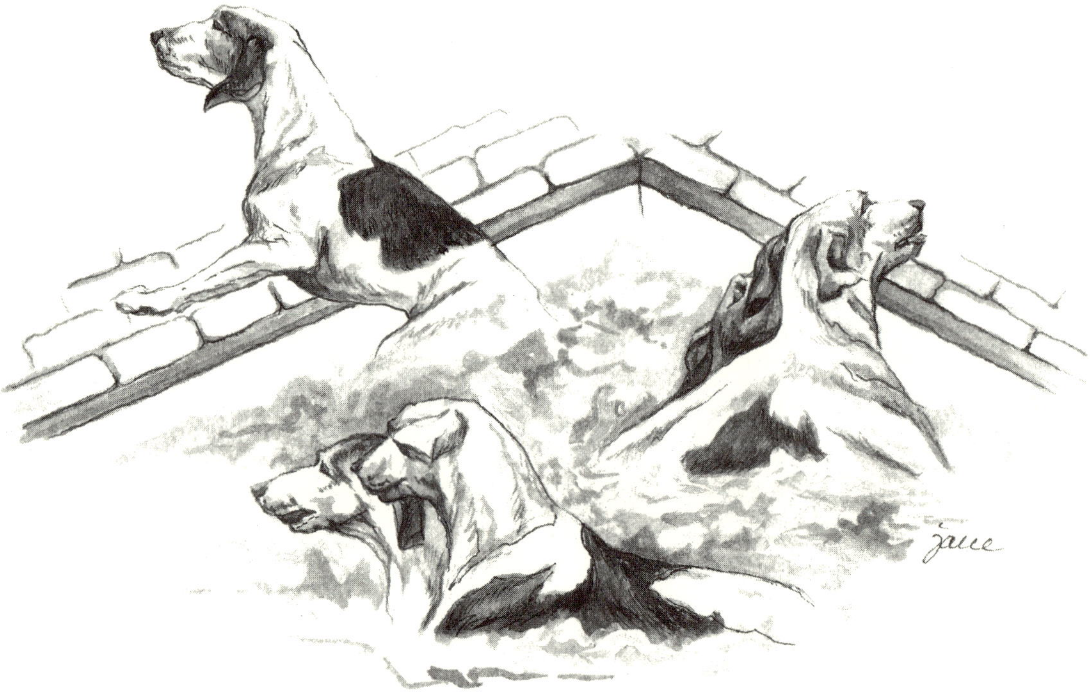

Opening Meet, from long standing, had to be on Thanksgiving, at ten in the morning. Usually we had a mini-drought during the 2 weeks before "The Day." By 10 o'clock in the morning—the hour at which we were to perform—the temperature was generally a mild 65 degrees after a low of 40 the night before. A blue, absolutely clear sky, with a brisk, east wind completed the picture. After riding around for 2 hours and jumping a few fences, everyone seemed happy to go home to family and turkey. Over the years I learned to accommodate myself to this situation.

One Thanksgiving things didn't go the usual way. For one thing, it rained the night before and we had a decent run. More importantly, our daughter's "significant other" was visiting our family for the first time. Doug, so far as we could ascertain, had no points of contact with the hunting world. I was worried that we could look like freaks from a different century in our scarlet coats—and abusers of wildlife to boot. At the meet, Doug looked inscrutable as he watched Susan ride off on one of our horses, after the blessing of the hounds.

The hunt over, we collected Doug from the car follower he'd been riding with and went home to our turkey dinner. There was some nervousness among us during dinner; it was a little like an interview. And, of course, since we knew Susan's feelings about Doug, we wanted to put the best foot forward. I've discovered since then that the day of car following was OK for Doug—not shocking—partly because he is an outdoor person, interested in nature, but mainly because of Susan and the way she looked in hunting clothes, mounted on a Thoroughbred horse.

But Doug is a careful person, and because he was in a strange setting, he was being especially careful about what he said. He was very straight-faced. I wondered whether the young man had much of a sense of humor.

At 2 o'clock it began to rain softly.

One of our major landowners had decided to "subdivide" a significant tract at the edge of his farm. I use quotes because this was not to be a subdivision in the normal sense. This one had "large lots," dedicated green space, trail easement. In short, it was to be so carefully done that we (the foxhunters) "would hardly notice the change."

At 2:35 the phone rang. I did not know the lady on the line well. She had only recently moved into the subdivision and was not interested in hunting. Did I know that a fox had been sighted a number of times sitting impassively on the bank across the street from the subdivision driveway, looking…at who knows what? Yes, I had heard. What if he is rabid? I assured her he wasn't rabid. Well, what was wrong with him? I explained about mange and how toward the end, foxes lose their fear of humans. And yes, it was contagious, but that healthy dogs, especially those wormed with ivermectin, seldom got it.

She got to the punchline: she had just seen the fox, had stopped the car and rolled down the window to look, and was amazed that the fox only slowly trotted off. It had made her nervous seeing a wild animal casually sitting on the bank looking at her. She had thought he was bedraggled from the rain, but maybe he didn't have much of a coat. And what was I going to do?

I thought about it. How long would it take to get to the kennel, load some hounds and get over there? An hour? The fox was dying of the mange and the various infections secondary to the debilitating mange mite…a

The Cat and the Swimming Pool

really crummy death—one of the worst in nature. Better to put his suffering to an end. The only practical way was with the hounds. I always handled it that way. It would be an adventure. Let's do it.

I told the lady I would be there as quickly as I could.

She said she would lock up her dogs, call all the neighbors and have them lock up theirs. So that by the time we got there, everyone would be inside, so not to worry. And would I call and tell her what happened, because now that they were in the country, they wanted to know all about what went on.

The four of us threw on raincoats, piled up into the jeep, went to the kennel, hooked up the trailer, loaded up eighteen of the oldest and wisest and headed for the subdivision. I figured that if I started at the point where the fox had been sighted and kept casting in ever larger circles avoiding the places a fox would obviously avoid, the hounds might get a whiff of the fox. And if that happened twice, in a line, so that I could catch the drift, that is, the direction of the track, I might actually trail up to the poor thing; it was clear he wouldn't run hard.

We arrived. After 30 minutes of casting, the situation appeared grim—after 45, hopeless. The whole thing had been a mistake. And we were getting pretty soggy.

I started back for the trailer. At the road, I paused, looking at the downhill slope where the houses were hidden in the woods. I thought we might give it one last shot—maybe he doubled back. I cast the hounds down the little watercourse. There was an almost-completed house 200 yards down the slope. The owners hadn't moved in so the fox might have run right past it.

One hundred yards down the hill, Ready raised his head and called. They flew to him. What a roar! And off they went, past the new house, down the gully toward the river, half a mile away. Time passed. I expected it to end any second as the poor dying fox was put out of his misery.

If anything, the cry became stronger, and the little voice in the back of my head started listing the possibilities for disaster implicit in the situation. It was pretty clear at this point that the quarry was not a dying fox. It was also not a deer, as those creatures had not yet arrived in that country. Obviously, a fresh, healthy fox. I was afraid that the hounds would drive the fox so hard he would swim the river, a development not without precedent. If that happened, we would have to make a huge detour and spend a miserable afternoon rounding up hounds: Once across the river, a fox had never been known to swim back.

Just at that point in my calculations, hounds turned and started back. Straight up the little gully, through the woods, coming right at the new house. We ran around the house, through deep mud as yet not landscaped, into the backyard. I had never been there before. The house was just another part of a dwindling hunting country. Not something to be explored. In the backyard, in a sea of red mud, there was large tree, spared by the bulldozer, and a swimming pool—full of water, transparent in contrast to the mud around it—heated, no doubt.

The cry was so wonderful that for an instant my fears were all calmed, and I stood, rapt, waiting for the red flame, the fox, to come licking up the bank, as he steadily pulled away from the hounds. And suddenly, I regretted that we were there, that we would startle the fox, that we would interfere, that the fox would throw up his head and see us and be afraid at our sudden intrusion and veer off and run away.

It didn't work out that way. Instead, a huge yellow cat flowed up the bank in that feline gait which most canine people think is somehow cheating because it is so fluid—dodged the pool—and without so much as a glance at the four of us, oiled his way up the tree to a height of 20 feet and ran out on a large limb for 3 feet and stood rigid—leaning forward, his attention riveted on the approaching sound. He looked irritated, maybe angry, his tail swishing as feline tails do.

My eyes went back to the sound in time to see the hounds five abreast and in full cry come up the bank running on their noses, without any thought about what was ahead of them except the strange track, the track of the cat, ever getting a little warmer.

The pool was 20 feet wide and 40 feet long, so it accommodated them all nicely. The whole area became a sea of red mud, the pool included—

with eighteen mature American foxhounds swimming in the middle. Ready and Satchmo had hit the apron a little ahead of the rest and gone down like submarines diving, or sailboats with too much sail running under. The rest having some vague awareness of disaster jerked their heads up and hit the water in a belly flop, as they tried to fly over the whole thing.

Well, what can I say? It was an awkward moment. There we were: wife, daughter, and prospective son-in-law trying to pull hounds from the pool before they drowned because they didn't know anything about pool ladders. And of course, as each one came out, there was a huge shower of muddy water. By the time we got them all out, we were soaked. Raincoats are not wet suits. Doug? I had forgotten Doug. Now he really would think we were crazy. He was covered with water and mud, looking from the cat to the pool to the hounds, with the kind of smile on his face that a person gets when he has made the "hunting" connection, no matter how weird the circumstances.

As we started around the house with the hounds, I glanced up at the cat. Still watching us. Tail still swishing. Faintly mocking eyes saying to me something about jumping to conclusions.

ᚠ

Cain's Song

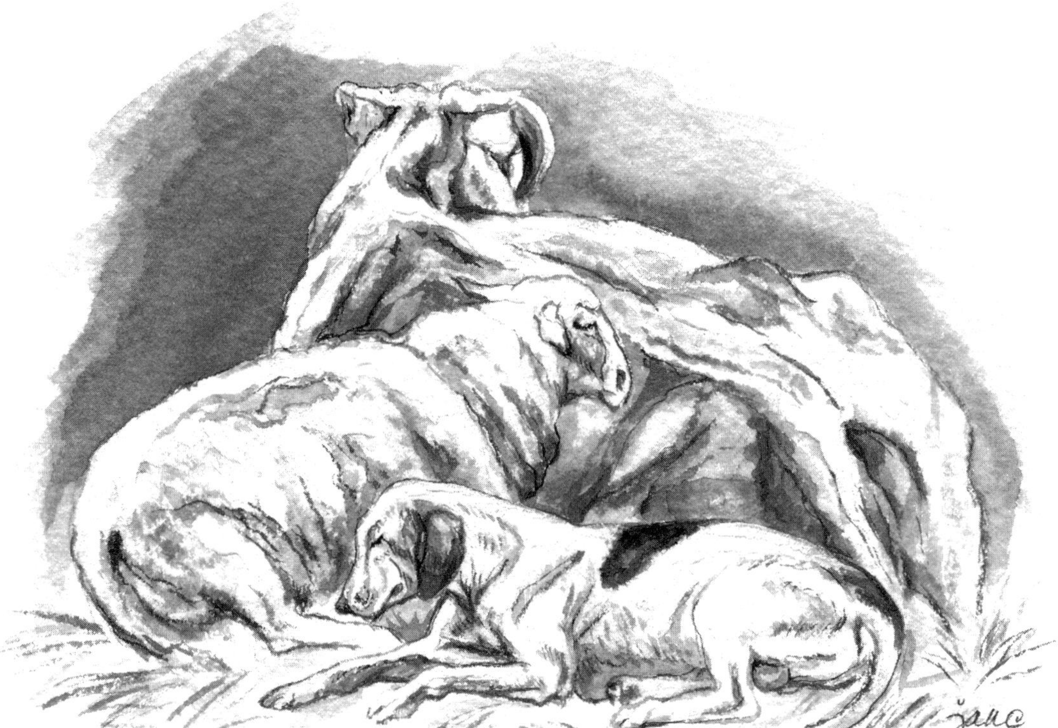

This is a dialogue in spirit between an old foxhound named Cain and a man named Cain. After the introduction, the hound speaks first, in italics. The man speaks in regular type.

Cain's Song

The room is dark.
The time is late.
No sound.
The eye adjusts.

Narrow light straight down
on cows and sheep and hounds.

Sleeping.

Amid the bodies of the hounds
in their straw-filled beds,
framed in yellow light
against peeling walls you
see his head—held back
as if in a great wind, shredded ears
flowing, muzzle raised
mouth slightly open.

The grey face glints
silver against the red coat.
Two scars cross above copper eyes
slit for distance, looking everywhere.
Looking nowhere.

Lost Hound

His mind becomes great
in its need. He speaks:

My name is Cain, and I am old.
Ten seasons I've seen—and rhythms slow
and the marks on my face and feet
encode the cost of joy,
record
the silent scratch of wire barbs
on flesh, unfelt in the moment's heat
when voice and the hot track merge
and the taste of blood from the brier-
torn tongue is sweet and breath is short....

Oh, we sang scent's song
my brothers and sisters and I—
sang the morning down
until time itself stopped, and scent
and song beneath a leaden sky
became as one....

...Stop! What right
have you to my name? And only
a hound at that.
    In the end I was no hunter, no
chaser of grass eaters, no chaser
of my own kind
(though once...yes once...in the time
of loss, fear reached for me, and anger—
I could not speak...and my brother died),
as you chase the fox.

Cain's Song

No! Nor herder of grass eaters...
Clean? They were all unclean, creatures
captive in the cycle of rain.
No longer prey.
They could not run.

But moved, always moving—
I was their slave.

And so I left them,
fled them—goats, sheep, camels—all
of them, left them, and they died,
for they were only eaters of grass.

And returned to the riverbank,
to the willow river's song—
to the soil. In my strength I
put hand to hoe. And in the morning
of the season, in my mind,
the furrows stretched before
me as if forever.
    And the bitter earth
yielded up her gifts as does the adoring
woman to the returning hunter....

I looked only at the ground
and thought myself
at peace.

But Brother Cain...could you sing?
Could you, Brother Cain?

Lost Hound

Could you at twilight at
the time of the first star
feel the night grow deep
around you and the others
as you enter the dark wood
alone…yet not alone?
Have you felt the earth's gift
of scent—rising
alive before you,
your secret definition shaped
in the prey ahead.
    Without eyes! only

the night?

    And the first whine,
the high keening of your sister, as if in pain,
but only the song's first sound, calling you.

Can you hear it still Brother Cain?
And the crash of baying voices in choir
like a mighty prayer:

'O Lord, of your mercy, let
the prey before us run forever,
that we may sing forever.'

Hear me, dog!

For I too once knew joy.
Yes, joy—
For she called me heir,
the first born.

Cain's Song

The laughing one. But in the end I was alone.
It was her garden, her loss, I was alone.
(The river
sings...still sings in the willow mist,
in my mind
at night. In my dreams
in the mist the river's voice
carries me away, but
I cannot move.)
I walked in silence.

But then in the morning of that day,
at the first
light, standing in the dust, I raised
my eyes, looked into
the blazing azure desert sun,
and saw my brother.

The bird!
Surely my brother.
Yes,
there! Airstrider in the surge,
on slanting wings,
washed in the wind. (Oh, the might
of him!) led aloft by the hand
of the wind. Our father, the wind.

(And the fierce utterance:
"Oh, to be
as my brother—
to be born aloft as he is:
by our father—the wind.")

Lost Hound

On that day the bird,
shatter-beaked and taloned,
slid—dove
down the dawn—cried
his sudden cry as a woman
cries her labor,
landed—embraced me
    spread his wings
as if in benediction above me,
spread his wings
as if in prayer.

In rage
I reached for the bird.
    My brother. Reached
in the strength of my arm to kill him—
betrayer—taker of the wind—
    our father
the wind.

And felt the depth
of talon clutch—the soft in-going
    of talons into flesh.

And saw the marks—
my name—etched
in blood upon my arm, against the blazing sky.
Then fear came and sat upon my shoulder.

And I
with arm aloft,
bloody name upholding—
knelt

Cain's Song

and killed him with my other arm,
his face unmade
against my knee…

Stop!
Let me speak, I must…
For I…
I, Brother Cain, knew
puppy joys, and the heat of her body,
and the tongue's curl
over the full tit. I pushed with puppy feet
against her breasts, and pulled her fullness into me.
I strove against her breasts
and won.

There were eight of us.
    We all won.

Lost….

But not all lost. Hear the voice
of the willow river.
Can you feel the place from whence
your mother came?
    Turn!
      Turn!
Brother Cain. Turn. For it is there
Within the willow river's misty song.
That which you seek. There.

But I cannot enter.
All is closed.

Lost Hound

No!
Leave grief!
Follow us.
Stand at the edge of
the willow wood—in the mist—
in the night with us,
this very night.
Listen!
And we
shall sing for you!

And though you bear
the marks of the son
    of the wind
cut deep
    into your arm,
we nonetheless shall sing.

The song will swell within you
as for us.
The heart-churn and throat-
tightening, will be for you,
as it is for us.

And when it is finished:
    the song spent,
    the night gone,
we will come to you at the edge,
where you may not enter,
and lie at your feet.

Cain's Song

On that day, Brother Cain,
we bring to you
our gift—unbidden:

Turn!
    Turn!

We will show you that
 which you have never
    known.

We will show you peace

    in our song.

ᚠ

Winter Run

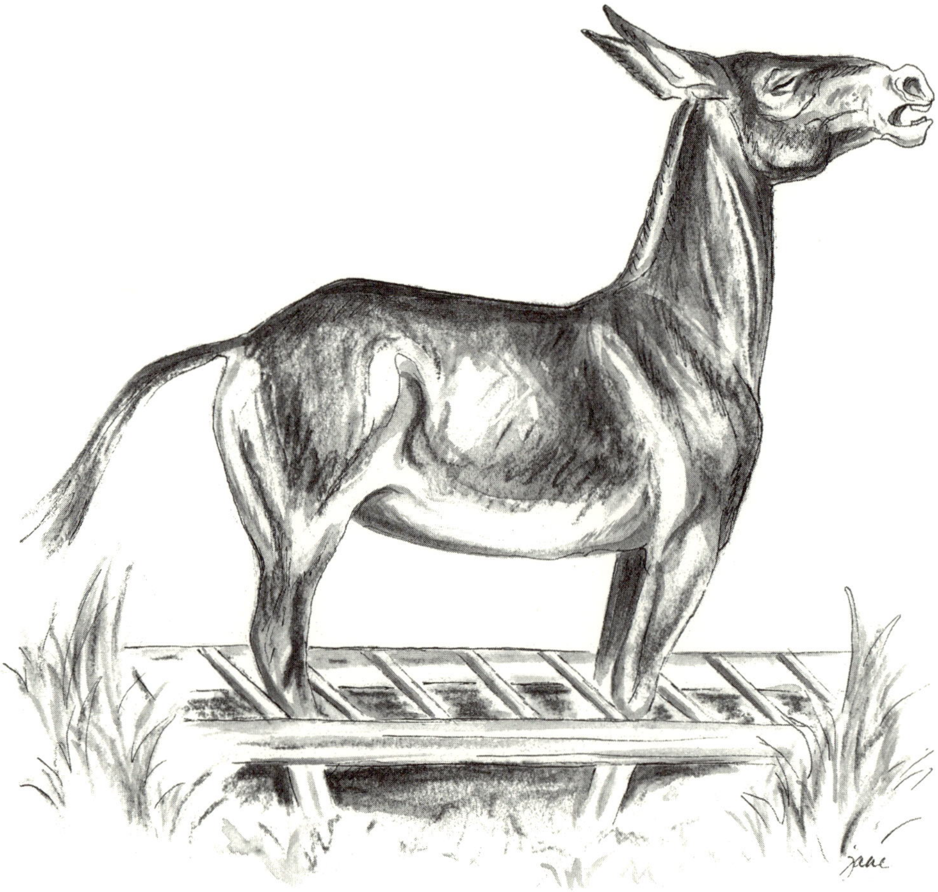

The land was old and acid and used only for grazing and garden plots. And because it hardly ever snowed in that part of Virginia, the color of winter there was usually reddish-brown. The fence lines had grown up in multiflora rose and cedars, and broomsage had become the main grass.

The farming wasn't much unless you were rich, but the hunting was good. During the war the deer had begun to come back, and now there was venison for special days. It was a time between times—although we didn't know it.

In 1948, the winter had begun in earnest in December and was so different and so bad that it was known for years after as the Great Winter. No one died—but a fuel-oil truck slid across a lane down the bank into the creek and stayed there for two months before they could get it out.

Deep paths had to be opened up through the snow so the cows could get water. And if you came from the cold into a barn insulated and made silent by snow, you made a sudden passage into a world so warm and so secure you might remember it for the rest of your life.

Between storms Leedy Waytes, who was a black man with nearly white skin, plowed out all the lanes in the neighborhood. He had a team of workhorse mares named Jewel and Queen. They were gray and tall and so strong they could pull the old wooden snowplow through the drifts so cars and trucks could get out.

Leedy also owned Old Bat, called Bat because she was blind in one eye, and Old because most people thought she was at least twenty-five, although Leedy swore she was thirty-five, and worthless. But that was just his excuse for leaving her all winter at Spring Hill, because every spring he came and got her and plowed all the gardens in the neighborhood, and charged people, too.

Old Bat was a brown mare mule whose body had begun to sag away from her absolutely straight backbone like a mountain shack whose ridgepole, against all odds, stays level as the shack falls in around it. But she was still spry and liked to escape from her pasture and go on rambles around the neighborhood. Strangers had been known to rush into the store in the village to report an escaped mule only to be greeted with a bored and cursory nod.

When she wanted to go somewhere, she walked up to the fence, cocked her head to get the distance, lowered her hind end, raised her front end, and hopped over—even if the fence was 5 feet high.

She was best known for her bray. It began with the usual mule whistle, but the second part was spectacular and sounded something like a tenor tugboat. In spite of being an extra animal to feed, her braying made her welcome at Spring Hill each winter because Professor James—who was a law professor and owned Spring Hill and was very eccentric—said that Bat's braying reminded him of the first cavalry charge at the Second Battle of Manassas. When Bat brayed at night, my mother, who had been raised in a convent, thought the old mule sounded like the end of the world.

Spring Hill was at the top of the hill. It was the home place in the center of a 600-acre farm, which was almost all pasture. We lived at the foot of the hill in a house my father had converted from a corncrib. We rented the house from Professor James. Both my parents were city people, but after the war they decided to live in the country. I took to it immediately—sometimes to their consternation, and often to their amusement.

My name is Charlie Lewis, and at the time I was eleven, and already very much in a hurry. My bonding with the land came about because

Matthew Weston was close at hand and was willing to take on an impatient white kid as a disciple.

Matthew and Taney were black and middle-aged and had no children. They lived in a cottage behind the house at Spring Hill. Matthew took care of the little home farm and the gardens, and drove Professor James. Taney took care of the house. She churned her own butter and rolled it with wooden paddles into those little round balls like you think you would get at Buckingham Palace—but she didn't like kids.

I spent all the time I could with Matthew. I was a nuisance, but it was his nature to be giving, so he put up with endless questions about the land and wildlife. He only sent me home once—when I set a pile of leaves on fire before he was ready.

After each storm that winter, when Leedy had plowed us out, walks to the village become an adventure. There were the tracks of possums and raccoons and foxes, and sometimes I saw the animals themselves, making their way down the plowed road rather than floundering around in the deep snow of the fields. Nearly every day, deer stood in the lee of a huge rock above the creek which paralleled the lane. When they saw me, they leapt up the hillside on their spring legs and disappeared in a spray of snow.

Then the dogs came into our lives—like that winter had—apparently from nowhere. At first, I was enormously pleased because there was the tingle of danger about them. They looked at me and ran, with their tails tucked and their heads raised, like wild animals, even though I whistled and called out. There were four of them. Nothing had been done about them because the snow was deep, and it was hard enough just to get the chores done, let alone try to kill wild dogs which disappeared whenever you looked for them.

When the first thaw set in, and it was easier to get around, the dogs killed two grown sheep at Jones's in broad daylight, while the family was shopping in the village.

A few days after the sheep were killed, I heard the dogs over the ridge behind the rock. Barking on the run—but not the long drawn-out note of the coonhounds. This sound was sharp and hoarse and staccato. Bat was on the other hill, with her big ears cocked, listening to them also. In the mist rising from the thaw, she looked all gray and weathered, like a ghost watching over the land.

The first dog, a tan long-haired bitch, came down the ridge, mute, and crouched beneath the overhang of the rock. Then a doe came into sight, panting and weaving from side to side, her tongue hanging out. The three dogs behind her were trotting, but still a little cautious.

The tan bitch shot out from beside the rock and grabbed the doe by the tongue as she went by, slamming into her sideways. Down they went, and the other three piled on top. The doe let out a long bleat as the dogs growled and struggled with her.

I crossed the creek on a game trail and edged my way up the bank for a closer look. When the tan bitch raised her head and saw me, her yellow eyes locked onto mine for a second. Then she rose up a little, pulled back her lips, and snarled from down at the bottom of her chest.

She scared the hell out of me, for a fact. I jumped back across the creek and ran down the lane and up the hill to Spring Hill, looking for Matthew.

He was milking. When I ran into the little barn and smelled the cow and heard her chewing and the milk swishing in the bucket, I came to my senses and blurted out what had happened. Matthew sat on the little stool, his hands on the cow's teats. As I told the story, he gripped the teats harder and harder until the cow flinched. But that was all he showed, sitting there in his own quietness, his leather baseball cap pushed back from his broad forehead.

When he finished milking, we got into the pickup and drove down to our lane, with the single-barrelled 12-gauge resting on the seat and floorboards between us.

"We've got to kill them!" I said. "Just like they killed the doe—don't we?"

"We'll see," he said. "Ain't much chance we can get around downwind without them seeing us. And anyway, the sons-of-bitches probably won't stay. Just kill and go after eating a little gut." It was the first time I'd ever seen him really angry or heard him use bad language.

At the turn, he stopped the truck. We crossed the creek and eased our way along in the shelter of the bank until we were close to the rock. Suddenly, he jumped up the bank, pulled back the hammer and fired at the tan bitch before I realized that the dogs were still there, growling and tugging at the carcass. He hit her—knocked her down for a second—but she didn't squeal like you would have thought a dog would. All she did was let out a sharp little bark, and they were gone before he could reload.

We stood there for a moment, silent, staring at the ripped open doe. Then he said, "C'mon Charlie, we got to skin out this deer, and I need you to help me."

When we were finished we loaded up the meat and the hide and drove the half-mile to the village and pulled into the parking lot, with the dirty snow piled all around. The potbelly in the store was glowing and people were talking before they went home. Matthew told the story of me and the doe, while everyone nodded approval.

Then Fred Ivory spoke up: "It's the snow what's done it, Matthew. What with not being able to get around the farm much less go hunting. But now it's eased up, and we got to kill 'em. You know about the sheep. Now listen to what happened to me night before last:

"Well, there I was, sitting, looking out the window, listening to the radio, and the moon full, and me just looking into the moonlight. And all of a sudden the cow in my back pasture threw up her head and took off with her calf, just flying, and me wondering what the devil's goin' on.

"Then I seen the dogs. They come across from my back fence. I got the gun and headed for the pasture. But when that tan bitch seen me, she give out with that little bark you talked about, and the whole bunch threw up their heads and were gone. But they come back in the night, because the next morning that calf was laying dead in the middle of a patch of churned up snow.

"They may be just dogs, but they've sure God gone bad, and we got to kill 'em, Matthew. I ain't never in my life seen anything like that tan bitch. She looks at you like she knows more than you do. And now that they can

Lost Hound

bring down a wild doe, running in a pack, Lord knows what will be next. Trouble is they ain't scared like wild animals. They just come and kill."

When Fred had finished, Matthew turned to Fred's brother Henry, who was the older of the brothers and was section foreman on the C&O railroad. He was tall and looked like a black Paul Bunyan. He wore hunting boots with his trousers tucked in and a stocking cap and a Mackinaw. The brothers dressed the same and looked the same, except Fred talked and was short. Henry was quiet—and he kept hounds. Hounds that would run anything you put them onto.

"Do you reckon it's eased up enough to bring the hounds in the morning, Henry?" Matthew asked. "I know where they're laying up." This revelation turned heads, mine included. Henry nodded and Matthew continued, "I'll get Leedy and Robert. You and Fred bring the hounds. The summer houses above Spring Hill is where they're staying when they ain't hunting. I seen 'em the other night and tracked 'em in the snow. You and Fred can walk in with the hounds, and we'll be at the three crossings; and if you jump 'em, at least one of us will get a shot most likely. The wind might be wrong, but we got to chance it. Maybe they'll run the country and not the wind."

Then he said to me, "Reckon your daddy would come, Charlie?" I said I was sure he would, bursting with pride that my Pennsylvania-born father, who was a virtual foreigner in that land, would be asked. But he had an out-of-character and uncanny ability with a .22. So, when precision shooting with no side effects was required, he was asked. Like the time a bat bothered a lady at evening prayer, and Daddy was commissioned to shoot the bat and not mess up the church. I remember him sitting in the front pew on the epistle side dressed in a Sunday suit, waiting, while the bat flew around and finally landed under the eave on the dark pine plate. And him bringing up the rifle real slow and hitching his body around to make the shot less awkward. And hearing his breath ease out. And the little crack from the short-short, and the bat falling dead. And me wanting to cheer, but afraid to because we were in church. Yes, I was sure he would come.

Winter Run

Matthew took me home. My father came to the door and stood there kind of skinny and awkward with the back light making shadows across his hawk nose and deep set eyes. Yes, he would be glad to come, and it would be fine to meet at the store at six. And yes, he agreed that something had to be done, particularly in light of the doe being killed.

It was a restless night—probably for my father too, because it would have been the first time in his life he had ever done anything like that. From the distance of years, I remember him as completely cool, but it is an unlikely memory.

When we got to the village the next morning, they were waiting around a fire they had built next to the hog-scalding tub at the branch. The hounds were baying in excitement in the hound boxes on the pickups. Besides Henry and Fred and Leedy there was Robert Payne, who was short and skinny and looked like a spider monkey. He drank some and had done time on the road gang, but whenever something big happened, Robert was always there. And of course, Matthew, who knew what to do, even though he'd never seen such a winter, or heard of a pack of wild dogs before. Standing by the fire, you could see the tension etched into their shadowy faces. It had been a long winter.

Henry and Fred and the hounds headed for the summer houses above Spring Hill where the ridge began which ran almost to the village. Robert and Leedy went to the crossing behind the barn at our house. They put my father halfway down the ridge, above where I had seen the doe killed. Matthew and I would be at the end closest to the village.

Matthew had Professor James's old double-barrelled 16-gauge. We crossed the creek and stood next to the rock outcropping at the end of the ridge. We couldn't actually see my father's stand, but sound carried well, so we would know what was happening, if they came our way.

At the other end of the ridge, across the lane from the summer houses, there was a rock pile, and that was where the dogs were spending the nights.

Henry said later that before the hounds were a hundred yards from the rocks, they put their noses to the ground and began waving their tales,

Lost Hound

showing that they had caught the scent of the dogs' night lines. They could see the bloody tracks of the bitch in what was left of the snow.

When the hounds started whining and pulling at the leads, the men turned them loose. Almost at once, they burst into full cry. Henry and Fred looked up to see the quarry crossing the lane in a tight bunch, heading south, up the wind, straight away from us. Two things saved the situation. The first was that they were heading for unfamiliar territory.

And the second was Old Bat. The dogs had veered a little to the east, and just as it looked like the show was over, or would never start, there came a bellow so loud that Matthew and I heard it at the other end of the ridge. There is nothing on earth that sounds as disgruntled as a pissed off mule. And Old Bat was really pissed.

Having escaped for whatever reason, Bat had decided to go a new way and had ambled down the lane toward the lake, which had a pipe cattleguard across it so trucks could cross but cows couldn't. When she got to the cattleguard, she walked right into the thing up to her knees and hocks and was stuck. And being a sensible mule, she didn't struggle, she bellowed. And that turned the dogs back to the north, heading downwind, toward us.

So with Old Bat bellowing, and the black and tans throwing their tongues like the end of the world as the hunt became a sight chase, my stomach jerked up into a knot which grew even tighter when we heard shots. Leedy and then Robert had let go with their single-barrelled 12-gauges and killed the first two. In spite of the shots, the last two kept running hard downwind rather than risk making the turn back into unfamiliar country. So they went right past my father, and next the crack of the .22 long rifle hollow point sounded and another one went down.

Which left the last one and Matthew and me, and him with the double barrel. It was the tan bitch. And as she rounded the end of the ridge, with the hounds in hot pursuit and the winter funneling down to that moment, she looked back and hesitated, as if to make sure the whole thing was for real, and not just a game, and couldn't we go home now. Matthew fired once, and this time she didn't get up.

Winter Run

As I held onto the sleeve of his old denim coat, trying not to cry, looking back and forth from the bitch to Matthew, I could feel the tension so hot in him I thought for a second he might shoot her again. But as we stood there watching the light go out of her eyes and the blood spreading around her like a snow cone, I felt him ease and saw his eyes change and soften. And when I looked again, she was dead.

The wind had stopped, and beneath the leaden winter sky the voice of a single crow filled the echoed silence of the morning. The hounds went over to smell the bitch's body, to be sure of what it was they had been running. When the others came up, there wasn't much to be said—running dogs with hounds had a bad feel to it, but at least now they were gone—and all that was left was to free Old Bat.

That should have been the end of it. But no one would let it alone. After all the versions of the great dog hunt had been told, and everyone had laughed at Bat's antics, we still didn't know where the dogs had come from, or how they had lived before they started killing livestock. Or how they had learned to run down wild deer, being just farm dogs. The questions lingered like the dirty snow from the winter, which we had never seen before either.

Spring came. And things worked back toward normal. Leedy went around the neighborhood plowing gardens with Bat, and to my disgust, I went back to school.

One day when Leedy wasn't using her, Bat, who was still living at Spring Hill, went for a ramble up to the summer houses. My mother saw her going and called the James's. Taney, who had the same opinion of Bat as she had of me, reluctantly agreed to find Matthew. Later that morning, he walked up the lane and brought the old mule back.

When I got home from school that day, I went to find Matthew and see if anything was happening. "C'mon, Charlie, let's walk up the summer house lane. I got something to show you." Bat was out for the second time that day, and we let her come ambling along behind us.

Halfway up, the lane cut through a bulge in the land, and as a result, there were 4-foot banks on either side. A dismembered deer carcass lay there, skewed and weathered. You could see the tooth marks on the long bones.

We stood silent for a moment, looking at it, with me holding onto Matthew's sleeve, again—and Old Bat right behind us, ears cocked.

"Leedy found a carcass like this over at Joe Steven's farm last week. Do you see what happened, Charlie?" he asked.

But I didn't. Not at first.

"There was a drift here between the banks," he said. "They run her up the lane, and when she hit the deep snow, she went down, and they caught her. Just like us, that doe didn't know nothing about no winter and deep snow. I don't reckon we'll ever find out where they came from, but that's how they learned to run down a deer. It was the snow what taught 'em."

And suddenly I could see it in my mind's eye: The tan bitch waiting at the foot of the lane, taking up the chase as the deer went by. And the other three, winded, beginning to flag. And her barking the sight chase, the deer running hard. And the final surge as the deer hit the drift and went down, the bitch reaching for the throat hold. And the other three piling on.

And then again: The hounds in full cry and Matthew with the double barrel, waiting, as the bitch rounded the little bluff and looked back—to be sure it wasn't just a game.

ᚠ

The Blessing of the Hounds

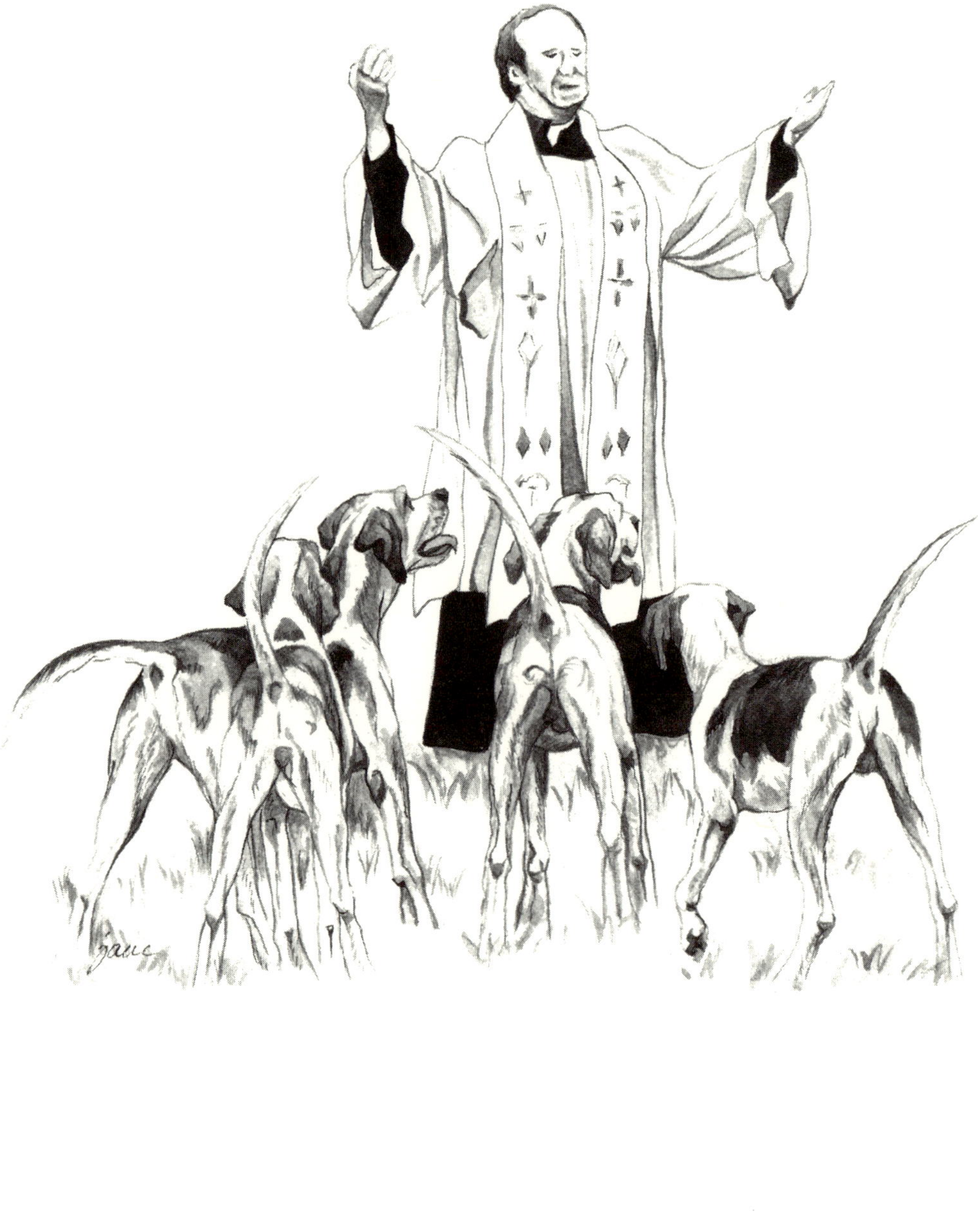

O Heavenly Father, you have in your creation knit together all the creatures on earth as in a seamless garment. Grant to us, therefore, on this our nation's day of Thanksgiving, the wisdom and grace to see all about us the works of your hand; grant that every one of us who looks into the eyes of horse or hound this day may see the reflection of your face; and grant that the skilled and cunning fox may be our pilot to a deeper understanding and love for your natural world;

+ Bless our solemn friend, the horse, who bonds himself to us in silence and does our will so freely.

+ And bless our brothers, the hounds, who guide us upon the chase and whose voices ring with such triumph and joy as to make an anthem worthy of your hearing.

And finally, O Lord, may all who participate today in this sport, ancient from time beyond reckoning, return refreshed and renewed in body and spirit to do your will for us. Through Jesus Christ our Lord, who with the Holy Spirit lives and reigns, one God, world without end. Amen.